SOCIETY WOMEN

SOCIETY WOMEN

A Novel

ADRIANE LEIGH

HARPER PERENNIAL

NEW YORK • LONDON • TORONTO • SYDNEY • NEW DELHI • AUCKLAND

HARPER ● PERENNIAL

Without limiting the exclusive rights of any author, contributor or the publisher of this publication, any unauthorized use of this publication to train generative artificial intelligence (AI) technologies is expressly prohibited. HarperCollins also exercise their rights under Article 4(3) of the Digital Single Market Directive 2019/790 and expressly reserve this publication from the text and data mining exception.

This is a work of fiction. Names, characters, places, and incidents are products of the author's imagination or are used fictitiously and are not to be construed as real. Any resemblance to actual events, locales, organizations, or persons, living or dead, is entirely coincidental.

SOCIETY WOMEN. Copyright © 2026 by Adriane Leigh Hill. All rights reserved. No part of this book may be used or reproduced in any manner whatsoever without written permission except in the case of brief quotations embodied in critical articles and reviews. For information, address HarperCollins Publishers, 195 Broadway, New York, NY 10007. In Europe, HarperCollins Publishers, Macken House, 39/40 Mayor Street Upper, Dublin 1, D01 C9W8, Ireland.

HarperCollins books may be purchased for educational, business, or sales promotional use. For information, please email the Special Markets Department at SPsales@harpercollins.com.

hc.com

FIRST EDITION

Designed by Jamie Lynn Kerner

Library of Congress Cataloging-in-Publication Data has been applied for.

ISBN 978-0-06-347392-8 (pbk.)

Printed in the United States of America.

25 26 27 28 29 LBC 5 4 3 2 1

Dedicated to all the women who turned their scars into weapons and their silence into fire.

ONE

Ellie

My eyes flicker open suddenly, the acrid smells of smoke and gasoline filling my nostrils. Something isn't right. I can feel it. Something is very wrong. Painful tears sting my eyes as I pull myself out of bed, my bare toes hitting the cool wood floor before another plume of gasoline fumes overcomes me. I have to fight the urge to bend over and retch. The hem of my nightgown hits the floor as I pad across the bedroom in the direction of the closed door. When I open it, my eyes struggle to adjust in the dim light. I can make out a figure standing in a cloud of smoke, the scent of gas overpowering as I blink once, twice, trying to make sense of what I'm seeing.

"Mom?"

The figure doesn't turn as she strikes a match and drops it on the chaise that sits in the corner.

"Mom?!" I cry, hot tears crashing down my cheeks.

Fire erupts, consuming the delicate fabric of the chaise in violent licks of orange and red. The flickering firelight catches her wild eyes, and then I see a serene smile curve her lips. I realize then what this is—this is her undoing. Our undoing. These will be my last moments on Earth as I suck in the last gasps of fresh air in the hallway.

"*Mom?!*" I wail, begging for her to see me.

She finally turns to me, whispering, "*You have to understand, baby. This is the only way.*"

"No—" But before I can move, the room is engulfed in darkness.

I jolt awake, gasping as my eyes travel the room in search of something familiar. I'm home. In my apartment. The one I share with my husband. This is not my childhood home. My mother isn't here. The flames aren't about to consume everything I hold precious. It was only a nightmare—the same nightmare I've been having since I was a kid. It's become such a presence in my sleeping hours that it's come to define my waking ones.

What I still don't know is if this is merely a dream—or is it a memory? Could something so violent, so consistent, really be pulled from the ether of my mind? I've been working with my therapist on exactly this—am I regressing every night to the helpless child I was back then? Or is my mind only torturing itself with fictional fears and traumas?

I turn in my bed, not at all surprised to find that the other side—the one usually occupied by my husband, Jack—is empty. The digital clock on the nightstand reads 5:40 a.m. I sigh, wiping the sleep from my eyes before rolling closer to the lamp to turn on the light. I grab the sleep journal that sits on the nightstand and begin scribbling in the details of my nightmare just like my therapist instructed me to do. I'm not sure what good it does, reliving my trauma each morning, the spike of cortisol and adrenaline that invariably takes hold as I write down the scene word for word. It's always about the same—my mother, the gasoline, the matches—but still I record every moment because I don't know what else to do. It's the only thing that makes me feel at least partially in control of my violent nighttime awakenings. At least this morning I didn't find a kitchen knife by my bed—that morning last week really shook Jack. Have my violent nightmares turned to terrifying reality?

I think of Jack—how he'd gone out of his way to find me the best therapist on the Upper West Side last year when my sleepwalking and night terrors took a turn for the worse. The year I turned thirty-two. The same age my mother was when she was committed to Mount Sinai—just a few blocks from here—and then Greystone Park Psychiatric, across the river in New Jersey, where she lived out the last years of her life.

I finish my entry in the sleep journal, then close it and get out of bed, my feet dragging as I get ready for the day. I stand in front of the bathroom mirror and take in my tousled, dishwater-blond hair and hazel eyes. My cheeks are too round and my lips are too thin; my jawline is broad and my forehead too big. I am the opposite of elegant and glamorous, and on my worst days I find myself wondering what my devastatingly handsome husband sees in me. He likes to say I'm a natural beauty, but I think he only says that to make me feel more confident. I do my best to dress smartly, to mirror Jack's more refined taste and style, but I always feel like I'm falling short in some way.

As I pull a loose-fitting pencil skirt over my hips and slip the faux-pearl buttons of my blouse through their holes, I think about my husband. I wonder what time Jack left this morning. I wonder if he never came home and instead slept on his pullout at the office. I wonder how long my marriage will last if my husband spends more time at work than in our ten-thousand-dollar-a-month corner apartment with a view of Columbus Circle, just steps from Central Park and a few blocks from Lincoln Center. I wonder what makes a good marriage and if I'm asking for too much when I beg him for date nights or romantic getaways. Lately, he only shows up for me when I'm on the verge of a mental breakdown.

These thoughts are still swirling in my mind as I walk into the offices of Northrup Thomas Investment Group an hour later. The company was started by my father, Daniel Thomas, before I was even born. It was the first place I worked after graduating from Columbia with a finance and economics degree, and it will likely be the last because when my father retires, I will inherit the business. In fact, I am the sole inheritor of my father's trust, and Jack is mine.

As the elevator climbs each floor in a satisfying rush, I trace the bruise on my wrist, my eyes following the inky blue and black colors fading to a sickening shade of yellow at the edges. I wish waking up with bruises was uncommon, but lately it's rarer for me to have unmarred flesh. The creamy shade of my skin is now always decorated with the evidence of my nighttime wanderings. Apparently, running into walls and doors and tables is par for the course when it comes to sleepwalking.

I adjust my computer bag on my shoulder as the elevator hums to a stop and the doors slide open. I step out, angling in the direction of the finance department and my corner office when my father's voice booms through the hallway. He turns the corner, a jovial smile spreading across his face when his eyes lock on mine.

"Ellie!" He wraps me in a warm hug. "Have a good night? Sorry I kept your husband out past his bedtime again."

"Morning, Dad." I suck in a breath, the scent of his familiar cologne filling my nostrils and easing the tension from my muscles. He must sense that I'm having a bad morning because he holds me for an extra few beats, squeezing my shoulder when he finally pulls away and catches my gaze.

"Jack told me you've been struggling with the sleepwalking lately—are you taking the medication the doctor prescribed?"

"No, I don't want to have to rely on Ambien just to sleep," I confess.

"If that's what it takes, honey—we can't have you walking around like a zombie." His eyes dart to my wrist, and he frowns as he takes in the bruise. "You know how I feel about this stuff, what with your mom and everything. I worry—Jack and I are both worried."

Then why doesn't he come home at night? I think, but I remain silent.

"No need to worry, Dad, I'm fine," I reassure him. If I were any other woman, I'd probably worry that my husband was having an affair, but I know Jack spends more time with my dad than with anyone else. They both find purpose in work—asking either of them to ease up would be like severing a limb, but that doesn't mean it isn't hard. I can't help but wonder if I chose Jack because he's familiar—because he's strong and protective, a cutthroat workaholic just like the man who raised me. But that's neither here nor there, and despite the nightmares that dog me sometimes about walking in on Jack with other women, I know it isn't true. I know it's just my anxiety and overactive mind getting the best of me. I'm grateful for the opportunities my father has given both of us—the fact that he hired us right out of school with salaries above and beyond our experience level has allowed us to advance faster and afford a two-bedroom apartment with a view of the park.

"You still having the nightmares too?"

"Sometimes," I say, in an attempt to downplay the frequency of them.

"Maybe you should take some time off, El—maybe a week at a beach retreat somewhere would do you good. Some juicing, some yoga—whatever women do to find themselves or calm their nerves or what have you." He delivers his words with a condescending smile. "You know these things run in the family, and this is just how it started with your mother."

"I know, Dad. I'm fine, though. Work helps distract me."

His gaze lingers long on mine before he shoots me that dazzling smile that wows investors. "That's my girl."

I force a grin, patting him on the back. "Maybe you and Jack should think about taking some time, though."

My father chuckles. "Haven't taken a day off in years and don't plan on starting now."

I smile. "Well, I should get to it, then."

"Sounds good, sweetheart. Shoot me a text if you need anything. I'm headed across town for a meeting with Jack at the downtown office—you know he's the best attorney in this city; you're a lucky girl."

I nod, waving him off. "I know, Dad. See ya later."

"Love you, El." He waves back, and then moves in the direction of the elevator bank. I smile, thinking how lucky I really am to have such a strong father figure in my life—even if he struggled to raise an emotional daughter. He did the best he could, especially with the fear weighing on him that maybe I would turn into my mother. That maybe madness is hereditary.

I finally walk through my office door, closing it behind me and dropping my computer bag on the desk before shrugging off my coat and sinking into the office chair. I sigh, thinking that a beach getaway really wouldn't be half bad. Then again, spending a week alone might be even worse than the solitude I'm forced to handle in the city with my husband at work all the time and my father's refusal to take a day off. Dad and Jack are the only family I have—and because my natural tendency is to be a homebody, I've lost touch with the few friends I had in college. I threw myself into work and spending time with Jack after I graduated from Columbia—that life doesn't leave much room for things like socializing. Jack even suggested I go to one of those speed-dating-like groups that are meant to connect people with new friends, but that just feels more pathetic than anything else.

A soft knock pulls me from my thoughts, and the door cracks open. "Delivery."

"Come in, Stacy," I call to my assistant.

"Hand-delivered. Must be important." She sets a sealed envelope on my desk, then leaves as quickly as she arrived.

I frown when I notice my full name written in elegant golden script. *Elyse Valentinja Taylor.*

I slip my engraved letter opener under the flap and open the envelope.

> *You are cordially invited to the Spring Women's Weekend hosted by The Society. Bedford, Westchester County, April 23–25.*
> *Business professional attire requested.*
> *Car Service Provided Promptly at 5:30 p.m. on the 23rd.*

I run my fingertips along the raised lettering. Is this invitation meant for someone else? I'm not familiar with The Society, so I do a quick internet search. My results are too broad, though, and even after putting in more details like "Bedford" and "Spring Women's Weekend," I come up empty-handed. I flip the invitation in my hand in search of any other details. There is no postmark, so I go back to the internet and try a few more search terms. The only result that's returned is a short article in *The New York Times* about a charity gala to support a children's literacy program. I scan the article to find a few familiar names of prominent New York families mentioned as members in the exclusive all-women's group. Accompanying the article is a small photograph of a group of a half dozen women dressed in elegant power suits in shades of cream and pastel. These women are clearly well-connected and poised, with perfectly veneered smiles and designer heels that cost more than my monthly rent. They embody everything that I lack, and may be just what I'm searching for.

Perhaps this is something Jack arranged and forgot to mention to me. I think how sparse my closet is, but going on a shopping trip before the weekend sounds like torture. I'll have to make do with the few basic pantsuits and pencil skirts I have.

I scan the words once more, glancing again at the front of the invitation to confirm it's really my name printed on it. I make a mental note to ask Jack when he comes home tonight if he knows anything about The Society—*if* he comes home, that is—and then I tuck the invitation in my bag and open my laptop to work on the quarterlies for Northrup Thomas.

TWO

Ellie

"Sorry I'm late, babe." Jack slides into the corner booth at our favorite restaurant that evening. "How was your day?" He leans over and plants a quick kiss on my cheek before spreading the cloth napkin in his lap and then sending me a tense smile.

"My day was okay—I'm glad tax season is done and dusted."

"I'm glad too, I think all that stress is exacerbating your . . ." He trails off, unwilling to say the words I know he's thinking: *mental illness*. "Have you thought anymore about going part-time? With that raise your dad gave me in January you don't even need to work."

"I *like* to work," I say, softly. Jack has been pressing this issue. I know he thinks the nightmares and sleepwalking are made worse by my busy work schedule, but I have a feeling my anxiety would get worse if I *didn't* have work to distract me.

"I know, baby, I know." He pats my knee under the table and gives me a condescending smile. "You are your father's daughter, through and through." He's being kind, but I sense something unspoken simmering beneath his words.

I think back on the first time Jack and I met at Columbia, warmth curling through me at the sweet memory.

Books go flying.

One minute I'm rounding the corner of the library's philosophy section, nose deep in a copy of Nietzsche for Beginners, *and the next I'm tumbling into the stacks surrounded by a ridiculous explosion of notebooks and index cards.*

"Oh—shit—I'm so sorry," a voice says, deep and smooth and unmistakably male.

His hand at my elbow, the only thing preventing me from falling face-first on the marble tile.

I look up and blink.

Because the guy crouching beside me—already scooping up my spiral notebooks carefully like they're made of glass—is definitely not some distracted freshman. He's older. Confident. The kind of handsome that makes your brain short-circuit a little. Tousled dark hair, warm brown eyes, strong jaw, expensive-looking watch peeking out from under a rolled-up sleeve.

He offers me a crooked smile. "Didn't see you there."

"That's kind of obvious," I say, wincing as I gather the last of my flash cards.

"Let me help—please," he says, already doing it.

His fingers brush mine as we reach for the same book, and something sparks in my chest, uninvited and inconvenient.

He hands me the copy of Game Theory and the Human Condition *like it's a rare treasure, then stands, shooting me a sheepish smile.*

"I'm Jack Taylor," he says.

"Ellie Thomas. Are you okay?" I ask, noticing the way he's rubbing his head.

"I'm fine. Nice to meet you, Ellie." His smile spreads, disarming and boyish. "I owe you an apology and maybe a new stack of index cards. Let me walk you to your dorm?"

I hesitate, glancing down at the mess I've mostly gathered.

"I insist," he adds, slinging his messenger bag across his shoulder. "You look like you carry the weight of five majors in that backpack. It's the least I can do."

I find myself nodding before I've even decided.

We leave the library together, walking into the late afternoon glow, and just like that, I'm doing something I never do—chatting with a stranger.

But Jack isn't exactly a stranger anymore.

He asks what I'm studying. I tell him economics and finance. He says that explains the flash cards. I admit I make one stack for every lecture. He grins and calls this "charmingly obsessive."

He's in his final year of law school. Wants to go into property law, whatever that means. He's from Boston, plays squash, quotes Hemingway without sounding smug, and laughs when I confess that I still don't fully understand compound interest despite having aced the exam.

By the time we reach my dorm, fifteen minutes have passed like a second.

I stop at the front steps. He does too.

"Well," I say, already fumbling for the keys in my pocket. "Thanks for not letting me marble tile back there."

He leans against the railing, eyes warm. "I should be thanking you. Best part of my day, bumping into you."

I laugh, half-nervous. "You sure you're not concussed?"

"No," he says, eyes lingering. "Just stunned."

Then, without missing a beat: "I'd like to see you again."

My heart lurches.

"What?"

He smiles. "You're smart, funny, and... probably the most beautiful girl on campus. I'd be an idiot not to ask."

My cheeks flush. I nod, almost on autopilot. "Okay. Yeah. I'd like that."

He pulls out his phone. We exchange numbers. He types mine in slowly, like he doesn't want to forget it.

"I'll text you," he says.

"Looking forward to it."

He gives me one last grin, then turns and walks away, hands in his pockets like it's the most casual thing in the world.

I stand there for a long moment, clutching my books like they're the only thing keeping me upright.

Jack.

What does someone like him see in someone like me? I don't know. But I can't stop smiling. Not even a little.

The waiter comes over, and Jack orders a gin and tonic for each of us and then orders our food. He doesn't ask me what I want because I always get the same thing when we come here. Grotta Palazzese is one of the few places we go for dinner because Northrup Thomas is a major investor and Jack is a firm believer in keeping things in the family.

"You'll never guess whose background check landed on my desk today." Jack's eyes search the other tables in the dimly lit dining room, as if he's looking for someone.

"Whose?" I ask politely.

"Jason's."

My blood runs cold. I sip my gin and tonic because I'm not sure what else to do. "Jason?"

"You know—Jason Hartfield. Surely you haven't forgotten him already? You said he had such a profound impact on your life—that's what you said, right? *Profound.*" Jack's tone is suddenly scathing.

My heart hammers as I consider my next words carefully. "Did I say that?"

"I believe so. Right after you told me you wanted a divorce. And right *before* Jason told you he'd met someone and was moving in with her. That's how the timeline went, right?" Jack's eyes finally land on mine. His normally warm brown irises are icy enough to make me shiver.

"I don't want to talk about it."

Jack sends a tight smile my way, adjusting his tie and then replying in a clipped tone, "Of course." The waiter arrives then, depositing another round of gin and tonics on the table. Jack swirls the alcohol in his tumbler, then takes a long sip. "I still wonder if Jason hadn't told you he'd met someone else if you'd have gone through with it—if you'd have divorced me and stayed with him."

I sip my drink, looking anywhere but at my husband. "I told you—we weren't . . . it wasn't an affair, Jack. Stop treating it like it was."

"It *was* an affair, though—an emotional one. You said it yourself."

"It was only a few months—we went to lunch a few times."

"*And* talked on the phone *and* you considered leaving me for him," he says.

I don't reply because there's nothing to say. We've gone over this a hundred times in the year since it happened. Replying would only add fuel to his fire, and Jack *always* wins. That's what makes him a great lawyer and a less-than-stellar husband, if I'm being honest. But we're still a good fit—I'm the yin to his yang, and even though I was wrapped up in Jason for a few months, I believe now that it was only out of loneliness and that my life has worked out just the way it was meant to. I wouldn't change a thing—even if losing Jason's friendship for the sake of my marriage was the collateral damage.

"I'm not hiring him—if you were wondering. Surprised he had the balls to even apply for the position after your dad transferred him to the Jersey office."

I still don't reply. If I leave Jack to his own devices, he'll lose steam. I'm starting to regret meeting him for a quick dinner before I head home and Jack goes back to the office for another late night.

We sit in silence for a few long minutes. The waiter arrives then with Jack's filet and my salmon. Jack nods once and then picks up his steak knife and begins to cut.

I shift topics. "Oh—I almost forgot to tell you—I got an invitation today from a women's group called The Society. Have you heard of them?"

Jack takes his first bite of filet and chews, shaking his head in silent response to my question.

"I haven't either. I'm not even sure why I'm on their radar—maybe it's something my dad set up. The party is in Westchester."

Jack's eyebrows raise. "Sounds like an interesting opportunity. When is it?"

"This weekend."

Jack swallows. Bites. Chews.

"They do a lot of charity work around the city," I offer.

He nods. "You spend a lot of time alone. Might be a good chance to meet some new friends."

"That's what I thought. They're sending a car service to pick me up Friday night." I take my first bite of salmon. "Although the idea of spending the weekend with a group of women I've never met before seems kind of weird."

Jack swallows, sips his drink, then nods. "I think it will be good for you. Get out of the city for a while." Jack bends, pulling something out of his laptop bag and setting it on the table.

"I have something special for you." His eyes sparkle with excitement, the anger over Jason apparently gone as quickly as it appeared. "Happy birthday, baby."

"Oh—I thought maybe you forgot."

"How could I? You're my favorite person in the world—if I could buy you the biggest diamond on the island of Manhattan I'd do it. I'd spend every day celebrating my favorite girl."

I nod but don't reply. His words don't ring as true as they used to, mostly because he spends all of his waking hours working, sacrificing us for his job.

"Thank you," I finally say, smiling.

"Open it," he urges.

I push aside the tissue paper in the gift bag, finding an envelope and a rectangular velvet box. I move to open the envelope first but his anticipation gets the better of him and he interjects, "That's a gift card for a weekend upstate at a juicing retreat. A guy at the office sent his wife up and she loved it. They have goat yoga, El; doesn't that sound fun? You're such an animal lover."

"Yeah . . ." I suppress a frown as I think about goats and downward dogs. I open the velvet box and my heart leaps when I find a pearl and diamond necklace with a dainty pavé-encrusted cross. "Wow, this is stunning."

"I thought you'd love it." He stands and comes around the table, moving my hair to the side and fastening the necklace around my neck. "There—picture perfect." He dots a kiss on the top of my head. "I love you, El. My world would crumble if you weren't in it."

"Well, we wouldn't want that," I quip, my heart heavy. I can't put my finger on it, but something about his words doesn't feel quite right. They're too manufactured, too perfect, too . . . *something*, and I can't help the sense of unease that bubbles through my system.

My father always told me if something feels too good, that's because it is.

I suddenly find myself waiting for the other shoe to drop.

THREE

Aubrey

"Thanks for asking me over tonight—I've been looking for an excuse to open this bottle of brut." I take two flutes from Ellie's wine rack and pop the cork on the bottle. I pour two generous glasses and then pass one to Ellie and sip from the other.

"Thanks for bringing a bottle over." She drinks from her glass, the fizz seeming to take her by surprise. Ellie's innocence is one of the things I like about her. She's one of those people who was coddled as a kid but not spoiled; I, on the other hand, had to fight for every scrap of an opportunity I was given, and a few that I wasn't.

"We should have girls' night at least once a week," I say, settling on the sofa next to her, thinking how easily she's allowed me to slip into her life since we bumped into each other in the hallway a few months ago. Ellie thinks our meeting was by chance, that I'm just another neighbor in the building, and it's in my best interest if I let her believe that.

"That would be great. This apartment gets so . . ." Ellie pauses, lost in thought. "Lonely sometimes," she finally finishes. I have a feeling she means all the time. I've noticed that Ellie's husband seems to avoid being at home with her, but I don't say anything. It's just one of the reasons I'm not interested in marriage: because men always leave, even when they vow that they won't. It's the way things go, like some unspoken catch-and-release rule. Men want the validation that you want them, and as soon as they have it, they move on to the next easy target. My existence is proof enough of that.

"Any luck finding a job?" Ellie thinks to ask.

I stroke the rim of my flute with my index finger, watching the city lights twinkle above Columbus Circle as I consider how best to answer. "Not yet," I finally say. "I'm weighing my options carefully. Thankfully I have enough savings to get me through for a while."

"What did you say your degree is in again?" Ellie asks politely.

"Environmental science," I lie. Ellie strikes me as the kind of girl who surrounds herself with high achievers; my college dropout past would only raise red flags. "I had big dreams to save the world as a kid, but it's a hard field to make a living in. Since my mom died—well, it's just been hard to focus on much other than getting used to life without her."

"I get that. My mom passed when I was a kid," Ellie informs me, as if I didn't already know. "I guess I don't remember much about grieving, but I do know it's hard to live without a mom."

I nod, letting Ellie's words hang in the air between us. "I've been thinking about going to a cancer survivors' support group." *Another lie.* In reality, sitting with a bunch of crying, grieving people sounds like the ninth circle of Hell. I force a sad smile and then add, "Maybe I could meet some friends."

"Oh—that brings me to the reason I wanted to invite you over," Ellie rushes ahead. "I got an invitation from a women's charity group for an event this weekend—do you want to come with me? I don't know anyone, so the whole thing would be more fun with a buddy."

"And you want *me* to go with you?" I ask.

"Yeah—well, I guess it sounds weird now that I think about it. We haven't known each other very long," Ellie says awkwardly.

"I guess it would be a good chance to get out of the city and make some new friends," I muse, pretending to be surprised that she's asked me to go with her.

"My thoughts exactly." Ellie drinks the rest of the wine in her glass and then takes the bottle from the coffee table and pours herself another. She's looking to drown her problems in bubbly tonight, and I'm all for it. I wonder how her husband would feel if he knew she was drinking like a fish before bed. Then again, how much does he really care when he spends all of his waking hours and a few of his sleeping ones at the office?

"How long have you and your husband been married?" I ask politely.

"Seven years in July—we've been together for almost ten, though. We eloped to Niagara Falls, then road-tripped our way around New England, and when we got back to the city we moved into this apartment and both started working full-time at my dad's company. We're in different offices, though—I used to think that was a blessing—who really wants to work with their spouse all day? But now that I see Jack next to never . . . well, sometimes I think working in the same office would have saved our marriage."

"Saved it? Are you having problems?" I drain the rest of the wine in my flute and then pour myself another.

"Just the usual things, I guess." Ellie shrugs. "Sometimes I think of his work as like his mistress. I didn't ask for a workaholic husband, but here I am, spending all my nights alone while he sleeps on a couch in the Financial District." Sadness hangs like a cloud over her.

"That must be hard," I reply.

Ellie nods. "Jack says I need to work harder to make friends, maybe get some new hobbies. He thinks it would help with the depression and sleepwalking and whatever. I know he's right, but I work a lot, and despite the fact that there's eight million people on this island, unless you're a barfly, it's hard to make friends."

"You're preachin' to the choir, sister." I shoot Ellie a reassuring smile. "Well, for what it's worth I think you should definitely attend that fancy party this weekend. There's no harm in checking it out, maybe make some new connections."

Her smile is soft, submissive. I see why a man like Jack likes her. Ellie is weak, insecure, easily controlled.

"I have a lot of social anxiety and I struggle in groups. But I'll go if you go with me," she replies. "Anyway, you fit in with high society women like this more than I do—maybe the invitation was meant for you." Ellie gives me a weak grin.

I nod, smile, then agree. "Okay then. I guess we have a party to go to this weekend." I take a deep breath, thinking how everything is falling into place so perfectly. "*To us*—making new friends in this godforsaken city."

"To us." We cheers and then each take a drink of our champagne.

Ellie doesn't realize it, but we're toasting to more than just friendship. We're toasting to a new future, to opportunities that promise to change both of our lives.

For better or worse.

FOUR

Ellie

"Elyse Taylor!" A woman approaches me, arms outstretched, as we enter the palatial Georgian mansion on Friday evening. I lean in for a hug, taking in the cloying scent of her expensive perfume and barely suppressing a sneeze. "It's so nice to officially meet you," she gushes.

I'm not sure what I expected on the hour-long drive up from the city, but it wasn't this. I feel hopelessly out of place among so much luxury. The woman's smile is wide and her golden blond waves flow in an elegant waterfall down one shoulder. I'd guess she's around sixty, but you wouldn't know it if it weren't for the faint crow's-feet around her eyes. I can tell she's the kind of woman who fills her schedule with Botox and facelifts and filler appointments in between her charity work and shopping trips to Bergdorf's.

"Hi—thank you for inviting me. This is my friend Aubrey Collins. I hope you don't mind that I brought a plus-one for the weekend." The woman's gaze flickers to Aubrey and she gives a quick frown before her measured expression returns. I'm suddenly embarrassed that I didn't ask about bringing a buddy along—but how could I? There was no RSVP number or contact information on the invitation. Besides, what kind of woman would I be if I agreed to a weekend away with a group of strangers without some sort of built-in support system? I may be naïve, but even I know better than to risk that.

"The Society is very exclusive . . ." Her icy-blue eyes narrow at Aubrey, a shrewd look crossing her face. "Bringing someone along is really quite bold and frankly untoward," she continues, and I wilt, thinking she might just send us back to the city because I've already broken some unspoken rule. Her gaze moves up and down Aubrey's form. "Well, I guess we can make do with an extra this weekend. You don't mind sharing a room, I hope?"

"Not at all," I say.

The woman's eyes flicker from cold to amused. "It's nice to meet you both. I'm Kat Volkov, your hostess for the weekend. Welcome to Bedford and my home, Tempsford Manor."

"Thank you for having us." I adjust the overnight bag on my shoulder. "I have to confess, I'm a little confused about why I'm here."

"Oh come, come. We'll talk about it over aperitifs." She gestures for Aubrey and me to move further into the house. "The ladies are waiting on the patio—they're thrilled to meet our newest recruit. We're very selective about membership. Only one new member annually, and the group's decision must be unanimous. How was your drive from the city? Paulo was prompt, I hope?" I feel my eyebrows rising. One new member a year? How on Earth did they choose me?

"The drive was great," Aubrey chimes in as we follow Kat to the heated patio that overlooks the estate grounds. The home is the epitome of old-world luxury: Italian tiles, an opulent double staircase, and marble pillars separating the various rooms. I've only ever seen homes like this in movies—never in real life. My father has a lot of powerful and well-connected friends and clients, but he made a point of keeping his business and personal lives separate when I was growing up. I found myself at home with a nanny most nights while he networked with movers and shakers around the city and sometimes around the world.

"Ladies," Kat coos as we step out onto the patio, "let me introduce you to Elyse Taylor—please give her a warm welcome into our little society. And this is her friend, Aubrey Collins."

"I go by Ellie, actually."

"Well, *Ellie*,"—Kat's smile is tight—"here we only use formal names. So much of the modern world has fallen into casual colloquialisms. The Society is an intentionally elevated experience."

I catch Aubrey's eye. She quirks one eyebrow, and I have to suppress a laugh, thinking that surely Kat is short for Katherine or something similar. I can't wait to be shown our room later and to giggle behind closed doors about this pretentious moment. But then, maybe Aubrey is used to a more elegant life than I am. I realize then that I don't really know much about her, despite the fact that I roped her into this weekend getaway with a group of strangers.

"Welcome, Elyse," the group of women chimes as Aubrey and I take seats at the outdoor dining table. I force a smile and wave, anxiety and discomfort settling in again.

Kat takes the next minute to introduce Aubrey and me to each of the women in the group—there are nine in all. Most seem to be within a few years of Kat's age, with only one being younger—somewhere in her forties if I had to guess. They're all poised and polite, just like Kat.

"We're so thrilled to have you in The Society," one of the women, Jacquelyn, says.

"Oh—I haven't agreed to join or anything, I just thought the invitation was interesting so—"

"Oh, honey, you're here—you accepted the invitation—that means you're in." Kat pats my knee under the table. The unexpected touch gives me a chill that I can't explain.

"Oh . . . I didn't realize . . . I thought I was just coming to check things out this weekend." I stumble through my words.

"Trust me, these are some of the most well-connected women in the city. Kathryn is the head of pediatrics at Mount Sinai. Jacquelyn and Susan have been at Goldman Sachs for thirty years—Susan is one of the first women traders in a man's world. And Martha has been the head of fashion merchandising at Bergdorf's for just as long—it's so inspiring. The connections and networking we can provide alone make it worth it," Kat says. "Events, fundraisers, galas—and every one an opportunity to climb the ladder."

"I'm not really into networking—I don't care about that at all, actually. I was just looking to make some new friends and maybe do some charity events . . ."

"Oh, you'll make the best friends of your life in The Society," Kat assures me. "And many of us have found a sense of purpose that was lacking before."

"If you don't join us we'll have an empty spot for the next year. We're all so stretched thin already—we really need someone to be boots on the ground for some charity work that we've had to turn down," Jacquelyn explains.

I pause before replying because it all sounds good—too good to be true. "May I ask—how did you find me?"

Kat's eyebrows rise for a moment before her smile grows. "Well, we have a selective nomination process and our membership is capped at a dozen members at any given time. We've spent the last year searching for just the right candidate after our last member moved to West Palm. Each of us nominates a few people we've come into contact with who we think would be a good fit with the group. Sometimes it's through social settings or work or even media coverage—Susan was nominated by Jacquelyn when they met at a work party years ago. Things just fall into place sometimes—you know how it goes. I believe in serendipity, don't you?" Kat says.

"So who nominated me?" I ask, feeling more confused than ever.

"Well, that was me. I came across your name in relation to your time at Columbia so I did some digging and thought your set of skills and talents would be a great fit for us." Kat smiles politely.

"My skills?" I push for more.

"Well, with finance and things." Kat's grin looks forced. I get the sense that I'm asking too many questions. "So much business talk—we usually like to spend the first evening catching up. It's been a few months since we've had a ladies' weekend." She turns to a sixty-something dark-haired woman across the table. "Tell us, Joan, how have you been since the last time we saw you?"

The woman—Joan—glances at her hands in her lap. "Not great."

Tears instantly well in her dark eyes before she takes a tissue from her bag and wipes at her face. "John has been distant since Savannah . . . left us." Joan sniffs, more tears welling. "I think we're both still in shock. I've been seeing my therapist twice a week and going to the grief group that she recommended, but it still feels so unreal. I still wake up every morning and have the urge to send Savannah a morning text message, and then I remember she'll never get it. That she's gone, my child is dead, and I'm supposed to just move on."

I sit in stunned silence, taking in the pain this woman has endured.

"It's still fresh, honey. No one here is asking you to move on." Kat pats her hand across the table.

"It's been six weeks since the funeral and it hasn't gotten any easier," Joan gasps. "It's like my mind refuses to believe the reality of losing her."

"That makes sense; there's no greater loss than the death of a child." Kat's face is the picture of sympathy.

"Especially when it's sudden," Jacquelyn joins in.

"But maybe I should have seen it coming. I mean—how didn't I? I know my daughter the best."

"That changes when they go to college, though—it's out of our hands then. They're surrounded by new people and living on their own for the first time..."

"Yes, but she was at Columbia. She was just across the city—we saw her most weekends. I should have known after the troubles she had." Joan cries softly. "She went through so much the last year."

"She went to Columbia?" I chime in.

Kat nods. "She was pre-law."

I feel Joan's anguish at the loss of her daughter coming in waves from across the table.

"I hate the man that did that to her—I think about revenge. I fantasize about hurting him—about taking everything from him like he did to me." Joan wipes at more tears.

My heart sinks as I realize there's more to this story than I realized.

"If she hadn't met him, hadn't been assigned to his class, maybe she'd still be alive."

"You can't think that way, honey," Jacquelyn says, attempting to console her friend. "We can't change the past; we can only impact the future."

Joan nods. "He deserves to lose everything. His job—his life. He needs to suffer for taking my little girl from me."

"He will—you have to trust that he will," Jacquelyn says.

Joan shakes her head emphatically. "I won't be able to move on until justice is served—I know it."

My eyes widen as I try to piece together the story. "Did a professor at Columbia do something?"

Joan's eyes lift, her gaze on mine, before she nods and sniffs. Kat speaks up then, her tone sympathetic. "Savannah was raped by one of her professors last semester." Kat swallows, letting her words hang heavy in the air. "She never recovered—her grades fell and she dropped out and . . . well, she suffered a lot. She committed suicide in February."

"Oh my God." Aubrey covers her mouth with her palm.

"I'm so sorry," I breathe.

"She reported him, but the university covered it up—it makes me so angry," Joan says. "We paid so much for the best education and sent them our precious girl, and they couldn't even keep her safe. I'd take down all of them if I could. The whole system."

"It's still a man's world, isn't it?" Another woman speaks up. Anger flashes in her eyes. "My sister was given a date rape drug when she was at a bachelorette party in Cabo in college. She woke up in a strange bed all alone—had to walk back to her hotel barefoot at dawn. It took her a solid year of therapy to be able to sleep at night. And of course, she had no memory of who did it. Just bruises and blood and knowing she'd been violated by a stranger."

"One of my daughter's friends was sexually abused by her boyfriend," Jacquelyn says. "They'd only been dating a few months, and he told her he wanted to marry her someday—that he couldn't picture his life without her—but one night he had a few drinks and things got out of hand. They were trying some of that dominance and submission stuff in the bedroom and he tied her up; she started to have a panic attack and begged him to untie her. He didn't. She cried. She told him to stop. He raped her. Said later he thought her tears were just part of *the scene*, whatever that means. Asshole." Jacquelyn shakes her head.

"And my daughter was turned down for a position in the company she was interning for last summer because she refused to fuck one of the executives in the company. It's disgusting the way some men seek power through sex," a blond woman across the table says.

The women around the table hum and nod their agreement.

"The world is so attuned to men," Kat says, shaking her head with outright disdain. "It seems impossible that they aren't all blissfully happy, but they aren't—they're miserable, and all they think about is acquiring more and more—power, wealth, control, women. It's so dehumanizing."

"And all women think they're different—think they can change a man or make him happy enough to rein in his appetites," a woman across the table adds. "They think that there are some things that will never happen to them, but they're all wrong. You know, I have a friend at *The New York Post*—I know she'd be willing to publish an op-ed. What better way to ruin a man than take down his reputation? The bad publicity alone would probably get him fired."

"He's tenured," Kat informs the group. "And he'll just deny it. The most disheartening aspect of this is that there are countless stories just like this one—of men going unpunished for these absolutely terror-inducing crimes."

"They're stealing lives, psychologically and literally," another woman says. The slow-simmering rage at this table is palpable. I listen carefully as the group discusses ways of helping Joan with her crusade for justice.

"I stopped in at the shelter on 77th last week and spent two hours listening to a group of women speak about the physical and sexual abuse they've endured. Oftentimes they're left to raise the children on their own while the men in this city continue with their promotions and business lunches at the Waldorf and run for political office, and"—the woman swipes at tears forming in her eyes—"it's disgraceful. I know the world isn't fair, but what is our justice system for if it can't protect the most vulnerable in our society?"

"Well, that's why we're here, isn't it?" Kat purrs, a strangely sinister smile crossing her face. "Those women need the support of women like us. They need someone to listen to their stories without judgment, someone to give them the opportunity to rise above their circumstances when the cards are stacked against them, women to teach them how to play the game when from birth the game is rigged against them. This is why our work is important." Kat turns to me directly then. "We balance the scales of justice and equality; we teach women how to control the power in a man's world—not just with time and donations, but with real action."

"How long have you been working with women?" Aubrey asks.

"Our first meeting was in 1979," Kat explains. "Our mission from day one was female empowerment and to provide a sanctuary for women who have had their voices stripped from them. You could say we've turned generations of women from victims to villains." She pats my knee under the table. "It's our calling. And we'd love your help reaching the next generation, Elyse."

Her icy eyes linger so long on mine that a dangerous chill courses through my veins. Kat's gaze feels more telling than any words she's uttered since we arrived at Tempsford Manor. I can't shake the feeling that if I knew what was best for me, I would decline the invitation to join The Society. I'd pretend this ladies' weekend never happened. But it's too late now—curiosity has gotten the best of me. Danger or not.

FIVE

Aubrey

"Well, that was intense." Ellie's eyes catch mine as soon as the door to our private room closes.

"They're like a cult of man-hating women. I love it." I can't help the excitement that bleeds through my voice. "Like vigilante justice in a power suit." I flop down onto the double bed by the window. "I wish that invitation was in my name—thanks for inviting me along this weekend. So far it's nothing like I expected."

"Me either. I expected canapés and Prosecco, but these women are on a mission to right the wrongs of the world." Ellie grins.

"It's empowering. Intoxicating. I'd give anything to be nominated for membership—you're so lucky," I say honestly.

"Am I?" Ellie laughs. "As cool as it sounds, it feels like . . . I don't know, a gang. Like once you're in you can't get out."

I wink and say, "I know, isn't it great? For so long men have had the exclusive clubs and access. These women are turning the paradigm upside down—quietly taking back their power in pearls and Louboutins."

Ellie tosses her duffel on the bed and then sits down next to it. "I don't have the wardrobe to even be seen with women like this. I feel so out of place."

"But they said they need someone to usher in a new generation of women—you're not like them, but that's exactly the point," I explain. "If you turn down this opportunity I will judge you so hard."

Ellie giggles, runs a hand through her dark blond hair, and then starts digging through her duffel. "Is it an opportunity, though? Maybe it's a death sentence."

"Well, that's dramatic," I mumble.

"Well, when you say it like that." Ellie laughs. "Thanks for coming with me this weekend. It helps to have someone to help me process everything."

"Of course. That's what friends are for." I give Ellie a hopeful smile.

"Some of the stories those women have are a lot to take in. Maybe that's why I've been a hermit these last few years—it's dark out there."

"You do kind of live in a bubble, working for your dad's company right out of college," I say.

"I've been blessed in a lot of ways, that's for sure."

"Nepo baby," I accuse Ellie playfully.

She scrunches her nose up at me. "Thinking on those women's stories kind of gets inside your head."

I nod. "You've been given a lot in life—it's your responsibility to give back now."

Ellie doesn't reply, and I think that finally my words have hit their mark. Women raised with privilege and access bubble wrap themselves from the real world, sometimes for an entire lifetime. Ellie doesn't act spoiled, but she is, just by the nature of the family she was born into.

"Feels like the more time I spend with these women and their stories the more I'll hate men." She lifts a pair of silk pajamas from her bag, fingering the tie at the waist as she seems to lose herself in thought. "Jack would die." She frowns. "He hates the feminist movement, says it drives men and women apart instead of bringing them together."

I shrug. "Maybe he's right, but so does rape gone unpunished. Don't you ever think it's weird that every woman knows another woman who's been raped or assaulted, but why don't any men know a rapist? Why don't they hold each other accountable? Why don't they warn women, like—*Hey, this guy was talking about some shady shit in the locker room; don't find yourself in a room alone with him.* Where's that warning?"

Ellie nods, still lost in her own thoughts. The sun is streaking the sky out the window in soft orange and pink hues, highlighting Ellie's wavy hair as she continues to play with the tie of her pajamas. She looks so innocent, almost childlike. I see now why The Society wanted her—not only her familiarity with Columbia, but she's soft, innocent, naïve, easily controlled. The same reason Jack likes her. The same reason I do.

"What are you thinking about?" I finally ask.

"Jack," comes her quiet answer. "Sometimes I wonder if he could cheat on me. He's rarely home. He works a lot so I don't know when he'd have the time . . . but the anxiety gets to me sometimes." I let her words hang in the air. "I'm probably just projecting. I had an emotional affair last year, and the guilt of it still weighs heavy on me. I'm lucky we're even still together—I told him at one point that I wanted a divorce. I'm glad we didn't go through with it. Jack has always been the constant in my life. His love keeps me stable. I started going to therapy after everything happened—the therapist suggested couples therapy, but Jack said he doesn't need it; he's not the one who cheated. I'm the one who's missing something, he says."

"Hm" is all I offer after her confession. I'm not sure what more I'm supposed to say. If she knew how much her husband really does need therapy, well, things would probably be a lot different. After all, would Ellie have cheated if Jack kept her happy and spent more quality time with her instead of working? Cheating is a symptom of a broken marriage, not the cause, and Jack plays a role in that whether he believes it or not.

"I'm worried the anxiety is getting to me—that I might reach a point of no return like my mom." Sadness flickers in Ellie's pretty hazel eyes.

"Why, what happened to your mom?" I ask.

Ellie shakes her head, unwilling to say more. I don't say anything else because I'm not supposed to know this part. But I know more than I've let on. If Ellie knew how much I know about her life with Jack, she'd probably cringe with embarrassment. But that's why I'm here: to be a fly on the wall, watch her like a hawk, and keep her on course. I thought keeping up the ruse of our new friendship would be easy, and it is, but I'm surprised to find it's also fun. I fit well into their lives—we make a neat little triangle, the three of us. Only Ellie doesn't even know it. But that's fine—the truth will be revealed in time.

SIX

Ellie

"So tell me about Columbia," Kat says as she holds a flute of Prosecco by the pool Saturday afternoon, her elegant legs crossed at the ankle and an oversize sunhat perched on her head. Even when she's relaxed her gestures are poised, her tone even. She's everything I could ever hope to be someday—a picture of grace that I will fall hopelessly short of achieving.

I push a hand through my wind-tousled waves and smile. "I enjoyed it. My dad is an alum so Columbia was a natural choice for me—I knew half of the staff by the time I was a senior in high school, and campus felt like a home away from home. Dad is a major donor."

"And your degree is in finance and econ?" she inquires politely.

"Mm-hmm." I take a drink from my glass, unsure of what else to say.

"Do you still have friends there?"

"I don't keep in touch as much as I'd like, but I attend events with Dad sometimes. They've renovated one of the buildings and are naming it after him—the dedication ceremony is in

August right before the fall semester starts. They asked me to give a speech, but public speaking isn't really my strong suit."

"What a nice opportunity. You should accept it—I'm sure your father would be honored."

"Oh, I don't have a choice," I say with a smile. "Dad would shame me into the next century if I turned it down. His public persona is everything."

"I bet. He sounds like a very influential man." She sips her drink, eyes lingering on Aubrey and another woman who are getting poolside massages. "That must be a lot to live up to."

I let her words linger between us before replying, "I've never thought about it, actually."

"Oh?" She tips her chin at me. "That's unusual."

"Is it?" I drink as I think about it.

"Well, most kids born with a silver spoon are taught to carry the weight of legacy."

"Oh," I say, "that's not my dad. He's too busy working to think about things like legacy. He's very driven—making money is his passion."

"More than his daughter?"

"I think so," I reply without hesitating. I've thought about this a lot—by the time I was twelve I knew I came second to my father's business.

"What about your mom?"

I gulp. The word *mom* feels foreign to my ears. This is something Dad and I rarely talk about. "She . . . wasn't a part of my life."

"Oh?" Kat says. She swirls and sips her sparkling wine, then levels me with her intense gaze. "Why?"

"She struggled with mental illness. She was institutionalized by the time I was five."

"Oh, I'm sorry to hear that." She gives me a sympathetic smile.

"Thanks. I don't have many memories of her. Not even any pictures. There was a fire that destroyed almost everything."

"Oh, honey, I'm so sorry."

"It was a long time ago," I say with a sad smile.

She nods, then finishes her wine. She lifts her empty flute in the air, and out of nowhere a gentleman in a crisp white shirt and black slacks appears to refill her glass. "Drink up, my dear. This is what the weekend is all about—connection and togetherness. It's the missing piece in our society today—I recognized it when I first founded our little group over forty years ago, and it's even more so now. Capitalism teaches us to consume to keep the wheels turning, but so much is lost in that paradigm. Profit over people, consumption over connection—it just leaves a terrible taste in my mouth. For that reason we try to have these ladies' weekends at least quarterly and more often if we can make the time for it." She smiles after the waiter refills my flute and then walks away. "The twelve of us are like family. It's always been that way, and now you're a part of the family too."

"I'm so honored," I reply.

I've only been here for twenty-four hours and already these women feel like home. Like a dozen doting aunts—a society of women with the sole focus of empowering and supporting each other. "I'm so happy you invited me. I admit I was hesitant at first—it was an unexpected request—I don't think I would have had the courage to come without Aubrey at my side. I'm pretty much a hermit when I'm back in the city."

"Oh, we'll do our best to change that. I've already got a few things in mind for you—if you're interested, anyway. It might feel a little out of your wheelhouse at first, but I think you'll find the work you do with us so rewarding."

"I think so too." I smile, feeling excitement course through me for the first time in too long. "I would love to help however you need."

SEVEN

Ellie

"Endless champagne, massages by the pool, and a private chef—I think we've stumbled into heaven on Earth." Aubrey waves one of the waitstaff over and smiles as he pours champagne into her flute. "I think I've been wine-drunk all weekend. If you don't join The Society I will, El."

I laugh. "I'm definitely joining—I was hesitant when we arrived but after this weekend, I'm all in."

"You'd better be—we couldn't be friends otherwise." She smiles. "I want to be your plus-one for everything, got it? Whatever events they send you to, I'm your wing woman, do we have a deal?"

"I promise," I say. "The weekend went fast—I can't believe I have to go back to work tomorrow."

"Have you talked to Jack at all?"

"We've texted a few times. He called last night but I missed it. I'm surprised he even noticed I was gone—he's been camped out at the office all weekend. I think he's just happy I've found a hobby and other people to spend time with so he doesn't feel bad for leaving me alone so much."

"Bleh—men."

"Elyse." Kat appears then, her eyes tracking between Aubrey and me. I get the sense she's been listening; I get the sense that this woman is *always* listening. "Take a walk with me."

My eyebrows lift before I catch myself and smile. "Sure."

I stand and she holds her arm out for me. We loop at the elbow and she guides me away from the pool and out of Aubrey's earshot. Most of the other women have left already—only Susan remains as she waits for her car to arrive to take her back to the city.

"I'm so glad we had the chance to connect this weekend," Kat finally says.

I nod. "Me too."

She trains her eyes on the woodline in the distance. "I wanted to have a word with you privately before you head home. I hope you don't mind."

"Of course not." I smile. We walk down a worn path that leads between two fields of wildflowers. A few cows graze in the distance, shaded by the trees that line one of the fields. Honeybees hover between blooms of tulips and violets and lilies. "It's so beautiful here, like something out of a movie."

Kat hums quietly, eyes focused on the path in front of us as a soft smile lifts her lips. "Isn't it funny how beauty and deadliness can coexist so peacefully?"

"Excuse me?" I think maybe I've misheard. "Deadliness? What do you mean?"

"Well, get too close to some of these flowers and it could be deadly."

"Really?" I scan the fields of beauty surrounding us. "Which ones?"

"Almost all of them." She catches the look of shock that crosses my face. "Oleander, snakeroot, the flower of the castor bean, even hydrangeas—so common in weddings—actually contain trace amounts of cyanide. And bleeding hearts contain properties capable of causing breathing problems and seizures. Even tulips have a poisonous sap that can cause rashes. The weaponization of plants is one of the few ways women have been able to wield power and exact revenge—especially within relationships—throughout history. Wives in India used a lovely white flower that had the nickname 'the devil's trumpet' for its deadly and hallucinogenic properties. All around us toxins are hiding in the pretty and the ordinary. Have you heard of Aqua Tofana?"

"No, I haven't." I watch a fat bumblebee bob and weave around a group of crocuses.

"During the Italian Renaissance, a woman named Giulia Tofana made makeup and perfumes, and one of her products, called Aqua Tofana, was a poison made with arsenic and belladonna—a beautiful purple flower with striking black berries. She sold her specialty to women in abusive arranged marriages, which were so common at the time. She was eventually caught and tortured, and she admitted to killing more than six hundred men over the span of twenty years. Wives would only need to add a few drops of the tasteless liquid to wine or soup and their husbands would get progressively sicker over the days from an ailment that seemed totally natural postmortem exams showed no sign of the poison."

A shiver courses through me. "Do you grow belladonna?"

"Of course, it's a member of the nightshade family—one of the most common plant species in the world. Tomatoes, eggplant, peppers—all are in the nightshade family. Most home gardens have at least a few nightshades. It's fascinating, isn't it? So many different flavors of evil and sometimes what's dismissed as simply pretty is really concealing the most sinister ingredients of all."

I nod, at a loss for words. These women aren't just regular, run-of-the-mill garden society women like they let on. Their focus on women's issues runs deeper than I anticipated. I hadn't considered all the ways women exacted justice throughout the course of history. Of course poison would have been one method, given their access to kitchen items and gardens and cooking, but it's especially chilling to think of it included as a tasteless addition to everyday soups and wine.

"I feel like I'm honoring all the women who came before me by growing these beautiful, toxic flowers. We don't need them anymore, of course—we have a justice system that's set up on the grounds of equality. Well, it's supposed to be, anyway. Plus, few of these flowers would escape a toxicology report now. We live in such an advanced world." Kat stops at the end of the path that leads to the fence that keeps the few dairy cows enclosed. She notices me watching them grazing in the distance. "We have goats too—there's nothing better than fresh goat cheese and raw milk. It's a shame it's not more widely available. Such a treat."

"Do you harvest honey too?" I ask, thinking of the bees.

"We have a beekeeper who comes a few times a year." She smiles.

"Tempsford Manor is so self-sufficient."

"Well, not even close, but it is nice to have the freshest ingredients. It's why I wanted to move to the country to begin with. I have a bit of a green thumb; I just don't have the time to nurture these things like I wish I could."

We remain silent for a few long moments.

"Well, enough of gardening talk—I wanted to touch base with you on something. The Society thoroughly vets all prospective members. I'm aware that you see a therapist on 57th for anxiety and sleep issues—I'd like to respectfully request that you keep all interactions and communications you have related to The Society confidential. This is crucial to our success, and discretion is the first requirement for all members."

"Oh." Anxiety spirals through me as I realize that somehow, despite the fact that my records with my therapist are supposed to be confidential, this woman knows more about me than she should.

"I need your verbal confirmation, Elyse," Kat urges.

"I'm sorry, of course The Society's secrets are safe with me . . ." I trail off because I can't help but wonder if *my* secrets are safe with The Society. "Forgive me for saying so, but I'm a little shocked that you know about . . . my private counseling sessions."

"I'm not sure why. It's effectively a background check—we need to know our members are dependable and stable. It's not any different than any other prestigious position in this city." She casts me a sideways glance. "Trust me when I say we learned the hard way that background checks and health assessments are a necessity for our organization."

My curiosity reaches a fever pitch, but I don't ask any questions.

"We would like you to attend a black-tie event this week with the aim of getting to know the Columbia professor who raped Joan's daughter."

"Oh." Shock vibrates through me. "I don't know how I could be of help."

"Your access is all the help we need. You're young, attractive, smart, I'm sure you realize by now that that opens doors, Elyse."

I don't respond because I don't think she wants me to. When she doesn't go on, I finally say: "What am I supposed to do when I get there?"

"Befriend him. That's it. We'll take care of the rest."

I continue to walk alongside her in silence. Of course this weekend comes with a price—the question is whether or not I'm willing to pay it. "That's it? Just befriend him?"

"For now." She smiles sweetly, but hidden behind her upturned lips is something more sinister. A chill ices my veins as her eyes hold mine an extra beat. "I can see your concern. You're sweet, Elyse, and men like him open up to women like you. We just need you to befriend him—The Society will handle the rest. If you're going to join us, you must trust us."

I nod, feeling all of the implications in her statement. If I don't do this, I won't be invited back. I will lose this network of supportive women. I'll be alone again, just me and that apartment and the ghost of my husband as he drops in for an hour a day before leaving again.

"Okay," I say, sucking in a breath. "I'll do it."

"Perfect. We're so thankful to have you with us." Kat pats my forearm, slowing her steps and then turning to face me fully. "You'll be such an asset to our team."

The Columbia event will be fun—if nothing else, having something on the horizon to break up the loneliness sounds nice. No more begging my husband for dinner dates and weekends away: I have my own plans now. And besides, I'll have Aubrey as a plus-one. Already hope is ballooning in my chest at the promise of our budding friendship. She lifts me up, gives me the backbone that I lack.

"Well, Paulo should be arriving to take you back to the city any time. On behalf of all of the women here this weekend, I want to thank you for coming. We are so happy to welcome you into our little society. We're turning over a new leaf, and we're thrilled that you're a part of it."

"You're sweet. I owe you a thanks for the invitation."

"Oh, don't be silly, dear. You don't owe us a thing—the pleasure is all ours." She pulls me in for a hug then, holding me tightly for long minutes, so long that my stomach prickles with the awareness of her closeness. The scent of her expensive perfume. The beat of her heart against mine.

Whatever I've stepped into this weekend, I'm beginning to think my life will never be the same. But I know more than ever that it's just the kind of change I need. If Kat believes that I can help them on their mission to empower women, then that's all I need to hear.

EIGHT

Ellie

You're just like her, aren't you?

Terror unfurls in my stomach as I reread the text message.

"Are you okay?" Concern pools in Aubrey's eyes.

"Uh... I'm not sure, actually." I frown. Aubrey leans over my shoulder to peek at my phone screen.

"Uh-oh," she says. "What's that supposed to mean?"

"I—I'm not sure." I swipe left on the screen, and the message vanishes as quickly as it arrived. "Wrong number hopefully."

Aubrey's eyebrows lift but then she seems to catch herself and steels her features again. "What time is your appointment?"

I finger the hem of the strapless cocktail dress that was sent to my apartment by messenger this morning. It's been three days since our weekend in Westchester—since I received my *first assignment*, as Aubrey has taken to calling it. "My blowout at the salon is at 5, I have makeup at 5:45, and the event starts at 6:30."

"The salon is right next to campus, right?" she asks, pouring a glass of wine for herself and then another for me.

"Yeah, I'm just going to change at the salon." I lift the glass, noticing my trembling fingers.

"Is it okay if I meet you at the salon later and we can walk over together?"

"Yeah, that works for me," I reply, my mind still lingering on the weird text message. I don't have time to think about it now, or ever really, but it occurs to me that deleting the message probably wasn't the best move because now I can't tell Jack that it happened—not with evidence, anyway. If I tell him he'll want to see the message, and when I don't have it to show him he'll likely just tell me I misinterpreted the meaning or that it was a wrong number.

"You look nervous," Aubrey comments.

I sigh. "I've been fighting butterflies since we got back from Westchester. It didn't help when the invitation arrived for the Columbia cocktail event, and then things really kicked up a notch when the box arrived with this little black dress."

"It's beautiful." Her eyes wash up and down the slinky satin fabric. "I'd take your place if they'd have me."

"I'd rather you were doing it," I say. I move to swipe my wine glass off the counter but I misjudge the distance and knock it over, causing the glass to crack into two pieces and blood-red merlot to spread across the granite countertop. "Shit!" I whimper. Aubrey wipes up my mess with paper towel, depositing the broken glass into the sink. I sigh, thinking how thankful I am to have her here. "I just don't know if I'm cut out for this. It's easy to say yes when Kat's in your face talking about empowering women—it's another thing when I'm sitting here thinking about all the ways this could go wrong."

"Please, Ellie, how could things possibly go wrong? It's just a few cocktails."

"Yeah, easy for you to say. You're not having drinks with a rapist."

"Well, there is that, I s'pose." She giggles, but I'm not feeling quite as lighthearted as she is. Her eyes meet mine and her smile softens to a frown. "Hey—I'm sorry. I don't mean to make jokes. Everything will be fine, I'll be right there. We can even have a secret signal if things get too much and you need to be rescued. What about . . ." She thinks a moment and then swipes two fingers across her temple. "Just make this sign and I'll be there."

That makes me laugh. "No, it's okay. I know it will be fine—this is my old stomping grounds. I'm just angsty because I haven't told Jack and events like this aren't really my thing."

"You'll do great, there's a reason they picked you." She pulls me into a quick hug, patting my back before holding me at arm's length. "You've got this. You have beauty and charm and brains coming out of your ears—there's no better woman for this job."

"Well, except you," I retort.

"No—not even me."

I shoot her a dubious smile. "Thanks for your cheerleading. You're the best."

"I know." She backs away, blowing me a kiss once she reaches the front door. "I'll see you soon, I'm gonna get ready and you're gonna get all glammed up and then we'll be off to the ball like two princesses."

She blows me another kiss, backing out of the door and letting it slam closed behind her.

I sigh, readying myself for what comes next. My first event as a member of The Society. If I didn't feel like a fish out of water before, I certainly do now. *Okay, El—get it together.* I shove the dress into my tote bag along with a pair of black pumps, then glance around the apartment a final time before heading out the door for my first appointment.

* * *

Ninety minutes later the makeup artist is putting the finishing touches on my look—a heavy winged cat-eye and a smear of sticky gloss on my lips to complete my new femme fatale aesthetic.

"Babe!" Aubrey breezes into the salon, a sexy red dress clinging to her frame. "You look incredible. I can't wait to see you in that sexy little black dress."

I suppress a groan. It's nearly go-time and I feel like a little kid on the first day of school.

"You're all set." The makeup artist spins me in the chair to face the mirror.

"Wow," I say. I've never worn makeup like this in my life. I wouldn't know how to re-create this look by myself, and I'm not sure I even pull it off.

"Let's go, let's go!" Aubrey spins my chair and thrusts my tote bag with the dress into my arms.

I turn to the makeup artist. "It's beautiful. How much do I owe you for the makeup?"

"Not a penny, it's taken care of."

"Oh, okay." I slip a twenty dollar bill out of my wallet and pass it to her for a tip.

"Thanks," she says, then tucks the bill into her apron pocket.

"Come on, let's get you into this dress." Aubrey pulls me out of the chair and guides me to the bathrooms. She stands outside a stall and waits for me to change.

A moment later I step out, shifting uncomfortably. "It's kind of revealing."

"Not at all—I think it's great."

"Thanks," I say halfheartedly.

"You should send a sexy selfie to Jack," she says.

"No way—he doesn't know anything about this."

"Would he be mad?" she asks as we walk out of the salon and head north on Broadway.

"No, not at all."

"So why not tell him?" she asks as we walk shoulder to shoulder down the busy sidewalk.

"I don't really know how to explain that I'm going to a cocktail party in the hopes of making conversation with a rapist. Doesn't really land well, ya know?"

"Yeah, I guess not." We walk the remaining two blocks to campus in silence, before moving to the west in the direction of the alumni building. "This looks like it."

We watch as elegant men and women shuffle into a glass-walled atrium that leads to the law library.

"God, this looks so fancy; is it too late to turn around?" I utter.

"Absolutely." She laughs.

I clutch my small designer bag, gathering all the courage I have before my phone chimes to life. I pause, pulling it out of my bag, looking for any excuse to delay the inevitable next few hours.

My heart stops when I glance down at the screen.

Black dress today. I like it. But green would really bring out your eyes.

NINE

Ellie

My mind is still buzzing with the second text message about the green dress as we linger inside the entrance. Someone is watching. Right now. Someone knows... something.

"I just got a weird text. It says they like my dress..." I glance from my phone screen to Aubrey's concerned eyes.

Her face falls. "Who do you think it is?"

My brain is flitting back through all of the possible acquaintances I have that might be responsible. Who could have seen me walking over here? Or worse—is it someone in the library with me right now? "I'm not sure."

She frowns. "Well, we can't think about it right now." She rubs my back, then returns her attention to the room.

"That's him," Aubrey whispers, interrupting my spiraling anxiety. She's standing at my side, champagne flute in one hand and her phone in the other. "It looks like him, right?"

I squint, glancing from the screen back to the man she's looking at across the room. He's standing at the bar, hip cocked and a whiskey tumbler in hand as he talks to who I assume is a colleague. "Maybe."

"It is. The hair is different, but look at the strong Roman nose. It's definitely him." She shakes her head. "Professor Matthew Ruehlman. What an asshole." She finishes her drink and sets it on the tray of a passing waiter. "Well, go get 'em, Tiger. I'll be here if you need me."

"God, I wish you could go in my place. You're such a natural at this charm thing."

"Nah, you're just a little rusty." She smooths a piece of hair at my temple and then taps my cheek with one crimson-painted nail. "You got this."

"No, I don't *got* anything," I spit back, suddenly annoyed that I brought her at all. I know she's here for moral support and she's only doing the job I asked of her, but I'm so tightly wound after the anonymous text messages I can't think straight. "Do you think they'd kick me out of The Society if I rescheduled?"

"Yes. Yes they would. I don't think there are a lot of opportunities like this one. You're only here because you're an alum, and it's not like they do these cocktail parties more than once or twice a year. You committed to this; you should follow through. Can you imagine the wrath of Kat if you didn't?"

"No, I guess I can't." I square my shoulders.

"Wait!" She puts a palm on my forearm. "Take off your wedding ring."

"Oh." My heart falls as I realize that of course I have to take off my wedding ring. Guilt spikes through me. I've never taken it off—not even in the shower. "Okay, here goes, I guess." I slide the ring off my finger and tuck it into my bag. I shoot Aubrey a quick smile and then head off in the direction of law professor Matthew Ruehlman.

My steps falter when the professor seems to sense me coming, his gaze shifting over the shoulder of his companion to land on mine. One eyebrow arches with interest, and I realize then what all the glam and the fancy strapless dress were about. My outfit does the talking before I do. I suddenly feel a surge of power course through my veins. I've never been the type that commands a room, but suddenly, I am. A sense of feminine pride wells in me.

I continue in his direction, heart in my throat when I'm finally close enough to meet him. I pause at his shoulder as if I'm lost.

"Can I get you a drink?"

I cast my eyes up to his—pools of melted dark chocolate. I nearly lose my breath as I take him in, at a loss for words in the presence of a man like this. Jack is handsome and direct but too busy for things like charm; Matthew Ruehlman commands attention. He has the look of a predator: unrelenting, hungry. My stomach twists in anticipation of what might happen next. I suddenly realize why people do this—go out to the bar and meet new people and engage in hookups and one-night stands. I'm in a world that I've never felt like I belong in and somehow I now . . . belong.

"Is something on your mind, beautiful?" His grin lifts at one side and my heart flutters.

"Y-yeah—I'd like a glass of whatever you're having."

He chuckles, eyes drifting lazily up and down my curves. I have to control my body's involuntary reaction to him. *He's a rapist*, I remind myself. *His actions took a young woman's life*. I will my beating heart to still as I keep this fact in mind while Matthew Ruehlman nods at the bartender.

"Two more," he says, before finishing his tumbler and sliding it across the polished bar top. "So what brings you here?"

"I'm an alum. Department of Finance."

"Oh, a numbers lady. I wouldn't have expected that. Not many of you around."

"What *would* you expect?" I step into his space. I'm so close I can smell his cologne. A wave of revulsion washes through me as I think about what this man did to Savannah. I think about Jack sitting at his oval desk in the Financial District none the wiser that I am here, attempting to flirt with another man.

"Hmm, pre-law maybe. That's my department. I wish I'd had you in one of my lectures—you're a sight for sore eyes. What's your name?"

I falter, wondering if I should tell the truth. "You owe me a few more drinks before I give up the details."

"Is that so?" He grins, leaning in, seemingly even more intrigued as I play hard to get. Is this what flirting is about? Never revealing the full truth? Verbal innuendo and building mystery and tension? "Well, I guess I'm one drink closer to getting what I want from the prettiest lady in the room."

He passes me an old-fashioned, giving me a half-smile. The ease with which he goes into seduction mode makes me want to vomit all over him. Instead, I take the drink offered and smile demurely. This man has game, but I can play games too.

"I'm Matt Ruehlman." He thrusts a hand out to shake mine. I accept, feeling the way his grip is purposefully firm and lasts a few beats longer than necessary.

"Nice to meet you." I avert my eyes from his penetrating stare. He's making me uncomfortable, and I'd be lying if I said I wasn't a little turned on at the same time. I hate my body for betraying my mind. I tell myself that underneath all this charm is a monster who takes advantage of young students.

I take another sip of my drink, feeling the bite as it goes down my throat. I'm not used to drinking like this—anything more than a glass of champagne or red wine is a lot for me.

He seems to be clued in to my discomfort. "Do you like your drink?"

"Yes—it's fine. It's good, I'm just not a big drinker," I admit.

"Babe!" Aubrey barges in at that moment, swiping my drink from my hand and downing it all in one swallow. "This party is lame, let's go to that restaurant opening in the Meatpacking District I told you about—if we catch a cab we can make it just in time."

"Let me call a car—I'll go with you." Matthew takes a step closer to me, as if to protect his prey from a threat.

Aubrey pauses, staring him down with a cold look all her own, before shaking her head and turning back to me. "Come on—*girls' night*—remember?"

I don't reply because I don't know what she's up to, but I'm thankful that she's rescuing me.

"Wait! At least give me your number." Matthew's palm lands on my elbow. Goose bumps erupt across my skin.

Aubrey's eyes lock on mine before she purses her lips and rolls her green eyes, gripping my elbow to pull me along with her.

"I want to get to know you—please—" Matthew's palm on my back stops me. "Your number."

I force a smile and then rattle off my cell number before allowing Aubrey to drag me out of the party.

"What was that about?" I ask once we reach the cool night air.

"You've got to keep them on their toes. The art of seduction is all about leaving them wanting more. Men are hunters—you have to make them work for it. You've just whetted his appetite. Trust me, our job here is done," she says as we head south on Broadway. "Are you okay if we walk? It's such a nice night."

"Sure." I take a deep breath, trying to calm my nerves as we weave through the throngs of people crowding the sidewalk. "Do you think he'll call?"

"Without a doubt, babe. You've got him on a string; I could see it in his eyes." She loops our arms at the elbow and winks at me.

I spend the next hour walking down Broadway with Aubrey, stopping for hot dogs and lemonade at a food cart and talking about the pompous arrogance that overflowed at the Columbia cocktail party. My feet are numb by the time we reach our building at Columbus Circle, but I'm grateful for the excuse to expend some of my nervous energy.

When I swing the door of my apartment open, I'm shocked to find my husband staring back at me.

"What *the fuck*, El?"

TEN

Ellie

"Have you been sleepwalking again?" Jack's eyes shoot from me to Aubrey and back again.

"No, it's not even ten o'clock—Aubrey and I went out," I defend.

His eyes narrow as if he doesn't believe me. It's not lost on me that he hasn't been home at a decent hour at all this week, and then the one night I go out, here he is, accusing me of . . . what exactly? I'm not sure. Anger sparks to life inside me, but I take a deep breath, trying to dampen it with the awareness that he's probably just concerned for my well-being. Especially after everything that's been happening the last few months.

"Well, have a good night, guys." Aubrey sends us a quick wave and then heads off down the hallway in the direction of her apartment. I wish she wasn't leaving. I like when she's there as my buffer, not just for fancy cocktail parties, but with my husband too.

"Night, Aubrey, thanks for coming with me!" I call after her.

Jack just grunts. I have half a mind to follow Aubrey down the hallway and leave this man to his own devices, but that wouldn't be very mature of me. And so I stand there, ready to take his verbal assault. Just like always.

"Why didn't you tell me you were going out? And what the hell are you wearing?" He looks me up and down.

"You don't like it?" I drop my bag on the table by the door and then twirl. "It's new."

He grunts again. "It's a lot. Plus the red lipstick—I hardly recognize you." He scans me over accusingly. "Where's your wedding ring, El?"

My heart sinks. I forgot to slip it back on my finger. "My fingers were swollen this morning—it was hurting so I took it off with some lotion."

He huffs. "A new dress, no ring, no explanation where you were tonight—it makes a man wonder what his wife's been up to."

"Is that so?" I kick off the satin pumps and head for the kitchen to pour myself a glass of wine. "It was nothing, trust me."

"Trust you?" His chuckle is rueful. "I found broken glass in the sink when I got home. I thought you were hurt, I thought . . . I don't know, I was worried. Where were you at?"

"The women's group I'm a part of had a gathering they wanted me to attend."

"Is that it?" he asks. *"A gathering?"*

He thinks I'm lying. Good, let him. Anyway, what am I supposed to say? I went to a cocktail party to land a date with a well-connected rapist?

"You're not going to tell me anything else?"

"Should I?" I pour some wine, take a sip, then tip my chin up at him. "Would it make you feel better to know where I am at all times? Like a little kid?"

"Yes," he admits. "I feel like you need someone to take care of you, especially lately. With the sleepwalking and the bruises . . . I mean, where are you going at night, Ellie?"

I don't reply. Let him think what he wants to. Anyway, Kat made me vow to keep everything that happens pertaining to The Society confidential.

"Maybe I should set up security cameras," he utters.

"Is that a threat?" I shoot back.

"Do you think it is?" he replies. "Jesus, El—I'm doing what I can to keep you safe; why the fuck do you have to make everything so difficult? How am I supposed to work and build a life for us when I'm always worried about you?" He finishes, watching me closely. The silence in the apartment feels deafening. "Maybe it's time for medications after all."

"What?" I reply.

"Just a low dose, just enough to help you sleep through the night. Dammit, El—every time I come home I search your arms for new bruises. I can't keep living like this."

"I'm not going on meds. We've talked about this," I say. This is not up for discussion.

"There's nothing wrong with a little prescription, something to take the edge off. It's not your fault, El—your illness is inherited." He takes a few steps closer, resting a hand on my shoulder in an effort to comfort me. "Listen, you came by your crazy honestly." He smirks but I'm not laughing. "Now I know how your father must have felt all those years with your mom and her struggles. It's damn hard to focus and provide for a family when you're worried your wife is going to undo everything you've worked for in one manic moment of madness."

My eyebrows shoot up at his words, but I let him continue to dig his own grave. He gives me a long look, as if he's trying to determine if he should say any more. "Babe—if you don't start taking something... well then, at what point are you orchestrating your own downfall? Left untreated maybe you're destined for the psychiatric ward too; have you ever thought about that?"

"Wow, that's a low blow." I get a sinking feeling as I let his words settle. I've always trusted this man with my life, but that was before sleepless nights and workaholism and run-of-the-mill stress took hold. While my husband may be direct to a fault, I've always thought he meant well. Is he right? If my mom had taken medication when her issues started, would she still have spent the last few years of her life in a psychiatric ward, forced into the confines of full-time care with no say in her future?

"I'm going to bed. Are you headed back to the office or will you be joining me tonight?" I finally say.

"I just stopped in to grab some client files; your father is expecting me back about now." He glances at his watch and then back at me, eyes softening. "I'm sorry, El—I know I get pushy sometimes, but I love you and I'm worried. You know that, right?"

Jack pulls me in for a hug. I gulp down the ball of frustration that's lodged in my throat and nod as he walks out. I love my husband—I love him with every fiber of my being—but moments like these make me think the line between love and hate is a thin one. It's something I never would have believed when we first started dating.

Thoughts enter my mind then about one of our first dates.

The sun is warm against my shoulders, and for once, New York's sharp edges feel soft. A breeze blows gently through the trees, carrying the scent of fresh grass and something sweet from a nearby food cart. Jack spreads the blanket on the lawn like he's done it a thousand times, every move easy and unbothered, like the world was made to accommodate him.

He looks up at me with that smile—wide, bright, maybe a little cocky—and pats the spot next to him. "Your throne awaits, m'lady."

I laugh, smoothing the skirt of my sundress as I sit. The fabric is light and floral, something I almost didn't wear because it felt too hopeful, too unguarded. But now, under the spring sky with Jack's eyes on me like I'm the only thing that matters, it feels just right.

He pulls a little Tupperware from the picnic basket and grins. "I brought the good stuff. Strawberries, brie. Sourdough I didn't bake, but let's pretend."

"I'm impressed," I say, accepting a strawberry from his hand. Our fingers brush—brief, electric.

"You should be. I scoured a Whole Foods at peak rush hour for you."

"And lived to tell the tale?" I tease.

"Barely." He leans back on one elbow, looking up at me. "But honestly, worth it."

He says it so easily, so earnestly, I can't help but blush. I glance away, pretending to study a dog chasing a squirrel across the quad.

"You've got this . . . glow," he says. "I don't know if it's the dress or the sun or just you."

I laugh, tucking a piece of hair behind my ear. "Do you always lay it on this thick?"

"Only when I mean it," he says. "And only with you."

I look at him—really look. His eyes are soft, sincere, crinkled at the corners from smiling too much. It's disarming. I'm not used to this kind of attention. I'm used to going unnoticed—being the quiet girl in the front row, the number nerd, the reliable daughter, the one who makes sense but never sparks.

Jack makes me feel like a spark.

"So," *I say, trying to sound casual.* "Last semester of law school. Busy year?"

He shrugs, unbothered. "Kind of." *And then:* "I've been seeing you around campus for a while."

I can't hide my surprise. "Really?"

"Yeah," *he says, picking up a piece of brie.* "Library. Econ building. That weird bench near Philosophy Hall you always sit at with your coffee."

I laugh. "You've been stalking me."

He grins. "Observing. With admiration."

I shake my head. "I honestly never noticed."

"That's the part that kills me," *he says, mock wounded.* "I can't stop noticing you, and you didn't even know I existed."

"I mean, I find that hard to believe."

"Well, it's true." *He turns serious for a moment.* "When I ran into you at the library . . . I swear, it felt like everything just clicked. Like the stars had been waiting for that exact moment."

I raise an eyebrow. "Now I'm starting to think you orchestrated that run-in."

He laughs, low and warm. "God, I wish I had. But no—fate was driving that day. I was just lucky to be in the car."

I smile. "You're very good at this, you know."

He leans in just a little. "Only with you."

And suddenly I feel like I'm floating.

I've never had a man look at me like this. Like I'm not just enough—but rare. Precious.

I lean back on the blanket, looking up at the sky.

The sunlight dances on my skin, and I think—for the first time in a long time—that maybe I really am lucky.

Maybe this is what falling in love feels like.

ELEVEN

Aubrey

"So Jack looked . . . upset the other night when we came home," I say, trying to tread lightly.

"To say the least," Ellie replies, as she swipes on her phone.

"Are you guys okay?" I ask.

"We're just going through a rough time," Ellie says, attention still distracted by her phone.

"Do you think he's the one?" I ask the question that's been on my mind for a while now.

"*The one?*" She laughs, then shrugs. "Is anyone? I don't know. Sometimes I wonder if I'm meant to be married at all."

"Really?" I've been curious about the same thing about both Ellie and Jack based on some comments Jack has made, but I'm not about to say it.

"Oh my gosh!" Ellie's dark eyes turn on me. "The Columbia prof just texted me!"

"Really?" I'm instantly dialed into her.

"Yep." Ellie's eyes dart across her screen. "He wants to go out Thursday night."

"Are you going to?" I glance over Ellie's shoulder in an effort to read the text.

"Yeah. I mean, I have to, right?" Ellie frowns.

"I guess if you're going to be a part of The Society you do."

She nods, working her lips back and forth nervously. "What should I say?"

"That you're looking forward to it would be a good start." I chuckle.

Ellie's fingers move swiftly across the screen before I watch her hit send on the text reply. "There." She smiles over at me. "I feel like a brand-new woman—I kind of like the challenge of getting this guy to trust me enough to bring him to justice."

I laugh. "We've only known each other a few months but I see a sparkle in your eyes that wasn't there before. You've turned over a new leaf and it looks good on you."

"Why thanks." Ellie's still smiling and I can't help but smile along with her. "Now, what am I going to wear?"

"You can borrow something of mine," I offer quickly.

"I might have to—my wardrobe is so boring compared to yours."

"Maybe The Society will send you something again," I say.

"Yeah . . . do you think I should tell them?" Ellie asks, setting her phone down on the kitchen counter and pursing her lips in thought.

"Probably," I reply.

"Okay, I'll send them an email." She picks up her phone again, navigating to her email app, when a new notification pops up.

"Is that him? He's eager," I say.

Her smile flickers to a frown. "It's Kat . . . or someone at The Society," she says, opening the new message.

> Sending something from Bergdorf's for you to wear to your next meeting with Matthew. Do whatever it

> takes to gather information from the target.
> Play to his baser instincts if you must. Report
> back immediately.

"Wow, they're treating this assignment like a military mission." I glance over Ellie's shoulder and scan the text. It's from an anonymous number. Convenient.

"Yeah . . ." She frowns.

I only shrug. "Has your stalker been in touch lately?"

Ellie sets her phone back on the counter and turns to me. "Nope. Maybe it was a wrong number."

"They mentioned the dress you were wearing at the Columbia cocktail party," I remind her.

"Right." A scowl twists Ellie's face before she turns to the fridge and pulls out an opened bottle of wine. "Well, maybe it was just a cruel joke. Hopefully it's all over now. And if it's not, I'll change my number I guess. Want some pinot?"

"You read my mind." I grin, pulling two glasses down from the wine rack that hangs above the kitchen counter. "All of your drama gives me whiplash. Fill me up."

"Same, girl. Same." Ellie grins, uncorking the bottle and pouring generously.

"Did you tell Jack about the stalker messages?" I ask, then lift my glass to hers for a cheers.

"And give him something else to nag me about? No way." We toast and then take our first sips of the chilled wine.

TWELVE

Ellie

"He's the monster, Ellie—not me!"

I wake, gasping for breath as my heart threatens to beat out of my chest.

"Fuck." I push my hands through my damp hair, taking a few deep breaths to try to calm myself. Maybe Jack is right—maybe I should try sleeping medication. How long can I really go on with these nightmares? My mind is torturing me every night, leaving me a walking zombie all day long.

I glance across the bed to where Jack should be. The digital clock on the nightstand reads 3:33 a.m. I pick up my phone and start to scroll, looking for any distraction. I soon find myself doing an internet search for the name "Savannah" and "Columbia University." Within moments I've found the poor girl's obituary. While it mentions nothing specifically about Savannah's troubles at Columbia, it does allude to a "difficult and ongoing struggle" that ended in a "peaceful passing."

My heart breaks as I read the words again, trying to make peace with the fact that the charismatic professor who flirted with me at the cocktail party is the same man who effectively took this young woman's life. My heart tightens behind my rib cage as I think of the way he came on so strong—did he say the same things to Savannah? Or did he just take what he wanted when he had the opportunity and then discarded her when he was finished? It occurs to me then that men like him never target women their own age—women who are confident and outspoken enough to take them on as an equal. Men like Matthew Ruehlman look for easy victims—young and naïve women he can overpower both physically and psychologically. Savannah was just starting to make her mark in the world before her potential was snuffed out by a predator.

Fire burns in my belly as I think about his irresistible half-smile and imagine him leaning against her, his dominant hands taking what was never his to take.

I then do a quick search for Professor Matthew Ruehlman at Columbia and find a treasure trove of accolades and articles. He's been teaching at Columbia for the better part of a decade; his staff photo is splashed across the internet, that same half-smile and intensely dark gaze just as powerful through a screen. I blink away the memory of his hand at my elbow, begging for my contact information. I begin to think of ways to retaliate, small comments and innuendos I can use to make him comfortable enough with me to reveal something—anything—that might help implicate him. I suddenly wish I could spend more time with the women in The Society, like a bad girl's boot camp, to help me extract what I need before this date.

By the time my search is over it's nearly six a.m.—time to get ready for work before I spend all day angsting over my date tonight. And then, like he can hear my thoughts, a text message pops up on my screen from the man of the hour.

How does Chez Daniel at 8pm tonight sound? Hope you don't mind the East Side.

I smile, texting Matt back quickly that the location sounds perfect. I even tell him I'm excited to see him and add a few exclamation points for good measure.

He replies instantly that he's excited to see me too and that he's going to spend the next fourteen hours trying not to think of my pretty smile. Always so charming, as if men like him can't turn it off. I toss my phone on the bed and then get ready for the day. I don't plan to answer his last text—letting him hang is the best option. I'm slowly learning how to play the game, thanks to Aubrey: Whet the appetite and leave them wanting more.

I smile as I get ready for work, thinking how nice it is to have plans for later. Even if my date is a criminal, at least he's an alluring one. After I'm finished washing my face and getting dressed, I add a swipe of red lipstick and smile in the mirror. I feel like a femme fatale, and maybe I am. Maybe it's just the kind of distraction I need right now.

Matthew Ruehlman is in for a surprise tonight, and maybe I am too.

* * *

By the time I walk into Chez Daniel on East 65th that evening, my feet are hurting and my eyes are aching with exhaustion from staring at a screen all day. I force a smile as the waiter informs me my companion has already arrived and requested a private table in the corner. My smile widens when I reach Matthew. He stands, placing a hand at my elbow and murmuring in my ear how beautiful I look tonight. I thank him for his thoughtfulness as I smooth the shiny black body-hugging dress over my hips. The box from Bergdorf's arrived at my office this afternoon, and I nearly choked on my own tongue when I realized how little it leaves to the imagination. Every dip and curve of my body is revealed, but then, I suppose that's the point.

To whet Professor Matthew Ruehlman's appetite without ever uttering a word.

"So how was your day?" he asks as we settle into the corner booth, side by side.

"It was great, outside of the nerves that kept me distracted all day."

"Oh?" He grins and slides closer. "Nerves about what?"

"This moment. Seeing you. You're quite distracting."

"Is that so?" He gives me that half-smile I've come to both love and hate.

"It is." I don't say anything else. I'm trying to play demure, like a naïve little girl he can easily control—as if his powers of seduction are already melting my defenses. My plan is to say little, smile often, and let my body language do the talking for me. I'm no expert at this, but I do know that the art of seduction requires mystery and illusion, and it's a game I'm more than happy to play if it means taking everything from this man and leaving him jobless and destitute. Justice isn't pretty, but I know my role, and while I did spend all day fighting my nerves in anticipation of this moment, it wasn't because I've succumbed to his charms; it's because I have a lot to accomplish tonight. Taking down a powerful man won't be easy, but nothing worth doing is, and it will be all the more satisfying when his life unravels before his eyes.

Professor Matthew Ruehlman has no idea what's about to hit him. He may think himself a clever Casanova, but I'm the black widow waiting in the wings.

THIRTEEN

Ellie

Girl! Give me all the details!

Aubrey's text message lights up my phone just as I'm climbing into bed later that night.

I smile as I type out a reply, a simple:

Not much detail to give. He was a perfect gentleman :\

Boo! comes her reply.

I yawn and stretch, setting my phone down on the nightstand just before the screen lights up with another notification. This time it's an email. I navigate to my email app and frown when I find a new message in my inbox.

> Elyse,
> Please reply promptly with any details that may be pertinent to the situation regarding the target.
> xxx K

I think over the conversation between Matt and me as we ate dinner. The date was short, ninety minutes at most, and my date talked about himself the entire time. I smiled, nodded, tried to play demure, but the conversation was mind-numbing at best. He asked no questions about me, which was for the best considering the situation, but if I had to be honest, I would say it was one of the worst dates I've ever been on. My reply to the email is short and sweet:

> No pertinent details to share. Sorry.
> —E

Before I've even set my phone down again, the app *pings* with another notification.

> Set up another date then. More intimate. We'll be in touch soon. xx

I groan audibly. Nothing about spending time with Matthew Ruehlman is easy, especially when I have an agenda beyond just getting to know him. I don't reply to the email, but spend a moment considering if I should text Matt and thank him for a great date. I decide to wait until morning. I don't want to appear too eager.

I set my phone back on my nightstand, thinking about my absent husband and how our marriage has gotten to such a deteriorated state. Then I blink away the tears forming in my eyes, thinking maybe one more glass of wine will help me sleep. Maybe I should treat myself to a mental health day tomorrow and book an appointment at the day spa on East 22nd Street. I could even bring lunch to Jack at the office like I did when we were first married. But then I think that's just another example of me overextending and him taking, taking, always taking.

I suck in a deep breath and wipe at more tears welling in my eyes. My phone chooses that moment to alert me with another text message. I smile, thinking it's probably Aubrey again. But when I pick up the phone something else awaits me.

You looked so beautiful today. I almost said hello.

A shiver of terror races through me as I reread the text message. Should I reply? Tell Jack? Call the police? The tears flow then, wetting my cheeks as frustration and fear flood my system. Helplessness weighs on my shoulders, and for the first time I think I can't trust anyone. Who is watching? Who has my number? And why?

FOURTEEN

Ellie

"Thanks for meeting me on such short notice," Matt says. He walks at my side, his shoulder brushing mine every few steps as we approach the shoreline of the lake in Central Park. We're only a few hundred yards from the busy city sidewalks, but it feels like a world away.

I lean in a little too close to him, smiling when he looks down at me. "I'm always up for a walk in the park with you."

"It's been a rough day—I had to kick a student out of my lecture for being disruptive. She kept accusing someone in the department of . . ." He trails off, as if thinking of his next words carefully. "Well, it doesn't matter." I remain quiet, hoping he'll reveal more. "It's always hard when a student isn't fully applying themselves, but come on, it's Columbia *fucking* University. Show up or go home, ya know?"

"Have you had to remove someone before?"

"A few times. And then I get calls from the parents and inevitably have to meet with administration. It's not a light decision but sometimes a necessary one."

I place an open palm on his shoulder and rub at the tension that's visibly overtaken him.

"Hey," he says, catching my hand and threading our fingers together, "what do you say we grab some takeout and go back to my place? I have a great view of the park from my apartment."

"Okay." I smile, always eager to please. I wonder briefly how a professor at Columbia can afford an apartment with a view of the park, but I don't ask questions. The email from The Society instructed me to arrange a more intimate date, and this feels like the perfect opportunity. He'll be more comfortable on his own turf—maybe I can get him to open up and reveal something that I can bring to Kat.

Matt pulls out his phone, taking a few moments to order a selection of food from his favorite Indian restaurant before we walk in the direction of the Upper East Side. I'm eager to see his place and find out a little more about him. Butterflies fill my chest as we near 5th Avenue—as soon as we exit the park together this thing between us becomes something else. Another layer of intimacy that can't be taken back. I'm not sure I'm ready for what might come next, but then, going back to my dull life before The Society feels unthinkable too.

Fifteen minutes later we reach his building just in time to meet the delivery guy with our food. I take a few deep breaths as we ascend in the elevator, nerves pummeling my system as we walk down the hallway with the scent of tikka masala in the air. I swallow the lump that's formed in my throat as Matt punches in the passcode and the door to his apartment swings open.

"Don't be nervous." He chuckles as he sets the bag of takeout down on the kitchen counter.

"Is it that obvious?" I sit on the barstool at the marble kitchen island, working my hands back and forth as he takes down plates from the cupboard.

"You don't have a very good poker face." He grins, then twists the cork from a bottle of red wine. He fills two stemless glasses, then pushes one to me before opening the containers of food.

"How was your day today?" he finally asks as he sits down beside me.

"It was okay—I thought about taking a spa day, but the more I relax and unwind the less I want to go back to work," I admit.

He nods. "I hear that. Even on the weekends I'm always reading essays or working on lesson plans. Everyone thinks being tenured is an easy ride, but the pressure is a lot sometimes."

I shift on my barstool as I think how his tenured position has protected him from prosecution for his crimes, but I can't dwell on that fact. I need a clear head if I'm going to make this man pay.

"Do you ever get away from the city for the weekend?" I take a sip of my wine, enjoying the way it warms my system almost instantly.

"Why?" he asks as he spoons food onto our plates.

I shrug. "To decompress, I guess."

"Nah." He shakes his head, then dips a chunk of naan bread into the garlic hummus. "Don't know what I'd do with myself. Relax by a pool? What's that?"

I smile, feeling a little more at ease with each passing moment. I understand why women are drawn to him. While our first meeting felt intense, seeing him in his own space is comforting. "Your apartment is beautiful."

He chews and nods. "Thanks. I bought it after I negotiated a bonus when I was offered a tenured position. Best investment I've made so far, financially and for my mental health. It's a bit of a hike from campus, but I don't mind—the view alone is worth it."

I follow his gaze to the floor-to-ceiling windows that overlook Central Park. Lush green leaves stretch to the north and south, and the Dakota building stands anchored at the opposite edge of the park. It's breathtaking. A thrill of pleasure runs through me at the thought of coming home to this view every day.

"You're a lucky man," I finally say.

"You'll get no argument from me on that point." We eat in silence for a few moments. My stomach is churning with anxiety—I have to find a way to get this man to open up a little more somehow. It's not like I can snoop around his apartment in search of some sort of evidence of his crimes.

"Do you want to watch a movie maybe?" he finally asks.

"Okay," I say, feeling like our chemistry is losing steam. We only had our first date last night. It's been less than twenty-four hours since we last saw each other—maybe I should have made him wait a bit longer to see me again. But I felt the pressure from The Society, so when Matt reached out and asked for an impromptu walk, I went for it. It's not like Jack will miss me at home anyway.

Fifteen minutes later we've finished eating, have packed away what's left of the food, and are nestled on the cream leather sofa together. I wonder again how a professor can afford a luxury apartment like this, bonus or no—polished wood floors, cathedral ceilings, crown molding, and modern furnishings dominate the space—but I don't ask.

Just when I'm thinking this second date of ours is going nowhere, his hand finds my upper thigh and he gives it a tender squeeze. "I really like having you here."

"I like being here," I confess.

He smiles back at me sweetly and a pang of guilt cuts through me. Can I really unravel all that this man has worked for? I muster a smile and then look away, his intense gaze weighing heavy on my thoughts.

"I really enjoy spending time with you," he says. "I know it's a little soon, but I couldn't stop thinking about you all day today." His hand travels up my arm and he leans in, his eyes focused on my lips. This is it. My heart hammers wildly.

"I . . . I need to use the bathroom," I blurt out.

"Sure," he says, smiling. "Down the hallway to the left." He taps my knee before I stand. "I'm gonna run the garbage down to the trash chute—I can't stand having empty takeout containers in the house."

I nod and smile. I take my time moving down the hallway as my thoughts race. I pass Matt's home office on the right and then find the bathroom on the left. I step in, standing at the door but not closing it all the way, wishing I'd thought to bring my phone with me so I could text Aubrey quick and ask what I should do next. I hear the door to the apartment thud closed and then, like a lightning bolt, an idea occurs to me. Without thinking twice, I leave the bathroom and cross the hall to the office. Everything looks orderly and neat, no stray papers or files, but my eyes land on a short filing cabinet in the corner. I cross the room and try the top drawer. Stacks of what look like student essays greet me. I groan, thinking I only have a minute or two before Matt is back.

I open the next drawer and find rows of manila files labeled with words like *insurance*, *retirement*, *taxes*, and *miscellaneous*. I snatch that last one and flip through it quickly, finding what looks like contracts and other legal forms related to Matt's work at Columbia. I groan—but then a check stub falls out. My heart clatters as I pick it up and flip it over to find the name *Savannah Walker* printed in the *to* line. *Ten thousand dollars* is scribbled in black ink in the amount section. My heart drops.

And then I hear the thud of the front door closing.

I nearly lose my stomach as I stand, tucking the check stub into my bra and then replacing the file and closing the drawer. I'm not sure what I've just found, but it feels like something. There's only one reason a professor would write a check to a student, and it can't be good. I wait a long moment as I listen to Matt move around the apartment. When he falls silent, I take that moment to peek around the doorjamb. The coast is clear, so I leave the office and cross quickly into the bathroom. I flush the toilet, flip the faucet on and wash my hands, and then leave the bathroom as nonchalantly as I can. When I return to the living room, Matt is sitting on the sofa facing the giant picture windows with the view of the park. Like a king looking out over his kingdom.

I settle beside him, leaving a little distance between us.

He closes the gap quickly, his smile soft and warm as he places his hand on my thigh again.

"Are you liking the movie?" he finally asks.

"It's okay," I say, thinking I haven't even been paying enough attention to remember what it is we're watching. Some geopolitical thriller with Ben Affleck.

"Thrillers not your thing?" he ventures.

I shake my head, unable to form words as I think about Savannah's name written on that check stub.

I'm about to stand and tell him it's time for me to be going when Matt turns to me, sliding a palm up to my neck and pulling me to him for a soft kiss. I submit to him easily, our lips moving together in a tender moment before his hands trail down to my waist, thumbs grazing the underside of my breasts. He tries to pull me into his lap but I resist before pulling away and smiling softly. "I'm sorry, I . . . I'm just not ready. I like spending time with you, but I'd like to take things slow."

Disappointment darkens his eyes before his jaw tightens. "If you're not ready, why did you wear that tight dress yesterday that left nothing to the imagination? You all about the tease?"

Nerves tighten in my throat and prevent words from escaping. I shake my head, unable to say anything. "Why did you agree to come to my apartment if you didn't want to fuck me?"

"I—I—" I don't know what to say, so I scoot away and stand, but he grips my wrist and pulls me back on the sofa with him.

"Come on, El—don't be a dick tease."

"I'm not—I just—" I try to yank my wrist away but his grip tightens. "Let me go."

His eyes flare, jaw flexing before he moves quickly, pushing me down onto the couch and crawling on top of me. Tears burn my eyelids as I try to push his broad chest away. I'm helpless. *This is what I get for going on a date with a rapist*, I think.

"Please, stop," I beg, pounding at his chest with my fists. He stops me, clutching both my wrists in one hand and hauling them over my head before he grinds his hips into my pelvis. It hurts, and the way he has me pinned is terrifying. "Stop it, please, please, don't do this."

He presses his lips against mine to shut me up, and I bite his bottom lip as hard as I can. I taste blood instantly and he pulls away, dropping my wrists to press a thumb to his lip. I take the moment of distraction to push and kick and thrash my way out from under him. I fall to the floor and scramble to my feet, launching myself across the room and toppling the coffee table as I do. He trips over it and falls to the floor before grasping for my foot. I lunge for the front door, yanking it open and running down the hallway screaming for help at the top of my lungs. When I reach the stairwell I turn to find the hallway empty. His door is closed—no sign of the monster who was chasing me just a moment ago.

Barefoot and shaking, I make my way down the stairs quickly. By the time I burst out into the lobby, I realize I must look unhinged—I'm barefoot and my hair is disheveled. Thankfully, the lobby is empty. I push open the doors of the building and suck in a deep breath. A cab is arriving at that moment. An older couple climbs out of the back, and I crawl in. "Columbus Circle, please."

The taxi driver looks me up and down a moment but doesn't say anything, just nods and then takes off from the curb.

The tears I'd been stuffing down finally fall in salty streaks down my cheeks. I narrowly avoided a sexual assault—I put myself in the same position Savannah was in, only she ultimately didn't make it out alive. I take a deep breath as I realize that whatever I just narrowly escaped was worth it if I can play a part in getting justice for the women who didn't make it out. If I can ensure he never does this to another woman again.

I just need to get home and send an email to The Society and tell them what I found: proof that this man is the monster Savannah said he was. I just hope it's enough.

My phone buzzes then and I pull it out of my pocket and glance at the screen.

Fucking bitch.

It's Matt. I open the message and then block him with a smile. He hasn't seen the worst of me yet.

FIFTEEN

Aubrey

"Ellie!" I pound on the door and call out, "Ellie! Open the door!"

The door swings open a moment later. Ellie's expression is alarmed. She doesn't say a word, just leaves the door open and turns in silence and walks to the sofa. She folds her legs under herself, eyes cast out the windows to Columbus Circle below.

"Are you okay?" I sit next to her.

She shakes her head but remains silent.

"Well." I toss the morning copy of *The New York Post* at her. "I take it you've seen this?"

"Seen what?" Ellie scrunches her eyebrows at me.

"Turn to page three." I nod to the paper.

She does and then her eyebrows lift with surprise.

"Oh my God." Ellie's eyes scan the article, which details every moment of her near-rape by the Columbia professor and includes a copy of the check stub made out to one of his students. Although Savannah's name is blurred out, the implication is clear. The author of the article also insinuates that Human Resources at the university was made aware of the professor's sexual transgressions with his students and covered it up.

"I can't believe they printed it," she finally says.

"I can't believe he almost raped you."

Ellie drops the paper on the coffee table in front of us and then leans back into the couch. Emotion hovers in her eyes, and she wipes her palms over her face. "I keep replaying every moment in my mind. I don't think I've slept more than a few hours since it happened last week."

My voice drops an octave. "Why didn't you tell me?"

"I just . . . couldn't believe it almost happened. I kept thinking about what it must have been like for Savannah. Every time I thought about it I started crying, so I just didn't have the words to say anything. I got home that night, sent an email to The Society with a photo of the check stub with Savannah's name on it, and I haven't talked about it since. Jack knows something is wrong, but I just keep putting him off and saying that work has been stressful."

I nod. I've been careful. I don't think she suspects anything, but I've been doing damage control as much as possible. I've stopped by every evening under the ruse of being a good friend, but really I've been keeping tabs on her. I knew when I moved into this place I'd end up seeing Ellie a lot more than I'd like to, but I didn't expect it to be this much.

"My husband would not be happy if he found out I was spending time with other men in an effort to destroy them," she says, sarcasm lacing her statement.

"Does he always have opinions on how you live your life?" I quip. It's weird playing both sides, gaining her trust and manipulating her thoughts—but I guess there isn't any other way to make things happen. It's been interesting getting to know her, anyway—we're nothing alike, she and I. It's refreshing and annoying all in the same breath. I like the challenge.

"He's going to lose his job for this. Especially since you've actually got evidence," I finally say. "The Society must be proud of their newest recruit."

"I guess," Ellie says. "I just hope he doesn't do this again."

"Men like him don't just turn over a new leaf, but at least he won't be able to prey on his students anymore."

"I didn't realize how much this job would affect me," Ellie admits.

"If it were easy taking down powerful men, we'd all do it," I say with a shrug. "You did good, El—you know that, right?"

Ellie nods. "I thought doing the right thing would feel good."

I pat her knee, a surge of sympathy welling inside me for her situation. Not only is she dealing with an absent husband but now she's navigating a group of the most powerful and well-connected women in the city.

"I got an email from Kat—she says she'll be in touch soon with another event invitation," Ellie says.

"Damn, these women move quickly," I reply.

"I just don't know if I have the heart for this again," Ellie confesses.

I let her words linger between us for a while before I finally say the only thing I've been thinking. "I wish I could take your place. Taking down these fucking assholes would bring me joy and purpose. Who knows how many women these predators would target. They're fucking untouchable and it makes me actually rage."

Ellie doesn't reply, but she lifts the paper in her hands and returns to the exposé on Professor Matthew Ruehlman. "He was such a dickhead," she finally says, "but a charming one."

"They always are." I think about Jack. If she only knew what I know. Someday the truth will be revealed and she'll realize just how untrustworthy men really are. "Want to order pizza from Pop's?"

"Sure," Ellie says, eyes still scanning the article.

"Got any red wine?" I ask, eager to get her mind off the misplaced guilt she seems to be feeling. She shakes her head no but doesn't say anything else. "Great—I'll have the delivery guy pick up a bottle on the way over."

She nods, her thoughts still a million miles away. This woman doesn't even realize that she's living in a gilded cage of her own making. But I'm determined to show her the truth of her small, pathetic life. There's freedom in honesty, even when it breaks us.

Especially when it breaks us.

SIXTEEN

Ellie

You left your door unlocked again. I could have let myself in last night.

I blink away my fear as I stare at the text message the next morning.

Wouldn't it be easier if you just let me in?

As soon as the next text comes I swipe left on the message and block the number. I've blocked every message so far, but it hardly matters when they keep coming from an anonymous source. I feel preyed upon; I feel targeted without any clear reason why. Is this random? Is this because of my father? Maybe one of his disgruntled employees—someone he fired at some point. Maybe even Jason returning to blackmail me after our affair.

My cell vibrates to life and another flicker of fear shoots through my veins. I glance down, prepared to find another message from an unknown number, when I see Aubrey's name flash across my screen.

Awake yet?

I don't reply, glancing at the clock to find it's nearly ten a.m. I never sleep this late, but I guess I needed it. Splitting the bottle of red wine last night with Aubrey probably helped. I crawl out of bed, wiping the sleep from my eyes as I stumble to the bathroom. When I'm finished, I pad on bare feet out of the bathroom and nearly run into my husband.

"Morning, sleepyhead." He plants a kiss on my forehead. "I was just about to bring you breakfast in bed."

"That sounds good. No work today?" I turn to the kitchen, headed to the fridge for some orange juice.

"Finally caught up on the Allegiance case," he says, referencing a company that my father works closely with. "You were dead to the world when I got home last night. Found two glasses and an empty bottle of pinot in the sink—who were you drinking with?"

"A friend," I say, my brain still groggy with sleep and maybe a little wine hangover.

"A friend, hm?" He pulls eggs and bacon from the fridge while I pour orange juice from the carton. "Seems like you've been hitting the wine hard lately—you sure that's helping with everything that's been going on for you?"

I narrow my eyes, watching as he cracks eggs into a bowl and then begins whisking. "It helps me sleep, so maybe."

He nods. "I didn't find any evidence of sleepwalking last night, so there's that."

I grit my teeth, pushing down the things I really want to say. Now would be the time to tell him about the text messages from the stalker, but I don't have the energy to be accused of being crazy and making things up this morning. Plus, I've already deleted them. I can't stand the thought of looking at them in my inbox every time I open my messages. I guess the smart move would have been to save them for evidence, but the truth is I just want them to go away.

"So who'd you share the wine with last night, El?" He's pretending to play it casual but I can hear the annoyance lacing his words.

"Aubrey," I answer.

"Really?" His jaw flexes with anger. "You like her?"

"She's kind," I offer. "You don't like her?"

He doesn't say anything, but his whisking turns aggressive. "I think you should be careful with a girl like that."

"A girl like that?" I nearly choke on my laugh. "What does that mean?"

"It means . . . I think she has an ulterior motive. I think she wants to break us up."

"Why on Earth would she want to do that?"

"I don't know, El, why on Earth does anyone do anything?" He grinds fresh peppercorns onto the eggs and then sprinkles them with sea salt. "You've been dressing sexier since you've been hanging out with her—the red lipstick, the late nights, the wine. You're becoming someone I don't know."

"Is that a problem? You just want me to stay the same sweet little college student you married?"

"Um . . . kind of." He drops a pad of butter into a warm skillet. It sizzles and melts instantly, and then he pours the eggs in after. He turns, facing me squarely. "You're becoming a stranger and someone I wouldn't even be friends with, honestly."

"Really?" I shoot back. "That seems dramatic, even for you."

"Even for me?" he scoffs.

I just shrug, thinking about what Aubrey said last night. *Does he always have opinions on how you live your life?*

"I hardly think I'm the dramatic one," he spits out, turning back to the eggs with a spatula in hand. He turns the heat down to low and starts pushing them around the pan. "Fuck—you always do this. Always try to make things bigger than they are. Can you blame me if I just want you to myself?"

I don't respond, because what is there to say, really? I know I've changed, but I like the woman I'm becoming. I feel a sense of purpose and belonging that I haven't felt before.

"You're not home enough to care, Jack." My tone is soft, submissive, just like he prefers.

"Nice—perfect. So it's my fault then? I work too much trying to support us and put some money away and achieve some of the goals and dreams we set for ourselves before we were even married?" His tone takes a darker turn then. "This is your fault, you know? Always fixating on my work stuff, but what part do you play in this, El? If our marriage deteriorates it'll be because of this—because of your fixating and constant anxiety and unhappiness no matter what I do. You're taking on too much—maybe it's work, maybe it's this new friendship, maybe life is just too much for you. But all the sleepwalking and outbursts and—fuck, you won't even talk to me about taking medications, and you won't admit that the sleepwalking has become a problem. What am I supposed to do? Just sit here and watch you destroy yourself? Now you drink bottles of wine at night to knock yourself out? You want to know what I really think? I think you're walking yourself right to the asylum with all of your bad decisions, especially considering your family history."

And there it is. The final death blow.

"You know what?" I am seething, feeling rage light a fire inside of me. My fingers start to twitch and my muscles tremble with anger. "You're a piece of shit. You're hardly the man I married, and it takes everything in me not to *hate you* for it."

Before I can think, I throw the full glass of orange juice in Jack's face. He ducks but not in time; the liquid splashes across his face and drips down his T-shirt, the glass landing on the floor and shattering into a dozen pieces. I turn on my heel and stomp out of the kitchen, Jack's growl of frustration following me as I reach our bedroom and slam the door, locking it behind me.

"Such an asshole," I whisper, trying to calm my clamoring heart. I think back on all the love that we used to share, wondering where it all went and when.

The sun is setting behind Low Library, casting everything in that soft, rose-gold light that makes even the sidewalks look romantic. We're walking slowly, neither of us in a hurry, our shadows long and overlapping as we move up the steps toward my dorm.

I can still feel the sun on my skin. Still taste strawberries and brie on my tongue. But more than anything, I feel him—his hand just barely brushing mine as we walk, like he's asking permission without saying a word.

I steal a glance at him. Jack's looking straight ahead, but his mouth is curved into that slow, secret smile. The one he wears when he's about to say something that will undo me.

I can't help it. I laugh, quiet and breathless. "Why are you smiling like that?"

He turns his head. "Like what?"

"Like you've got a secret."

"Maybe I do."

"Oh yeah?"

He stops walking. We're halfway up the steps, the hum of the city below us, but here it's just the two of us—like the air has gone still, waiting.

He looks at me for a long moment. Not intense, not aggressive. Just open. Like I'm the answer to something he didn't know he was searching for.

Then he says, "I was thinking about kissing you."

My breath catches. My heart hammers. I manage a soft, nervous laugh. "Were you?"

He steps a little closer. "Yeah. I have been since the minute you ran into me in the library. But now . . . I really want to."

My cheeks are burning, but I don't look away. I'm standing completely still. My lips parted, my pulse fluttering like bird wings in my throat.

"Well," I whisper. "What are you waiting for?"

His hand brushes my cheek, fingers grazing the edge of my jaw. It's the kind of touch that asks—is this okay?—even if his mouth doesn't say it.

And I nod. Just once.

Then he leans in.

The kiss is slow. Careful. Like he's memorizing it as he goes. His lips are warm, the faint taste of champagne and summer on his breath. I melt into it without thinking, without fear. Just feeling.

The moment stretches—weightless and golden— and when he finally pulls back, I'm breathless and smiling, blinking up at him like I've just stepped out of a dream.

"Wow," he says softly, forehead resting against mine. "That was even better than I imagined."

I laugh again—a real, bubbling sound that I didn't know I was holding in. "You imagine things like this often?"

He grins. "Only with you."

I look at him—this boy with the movie-star smile and the steady hands, the upperclassman who somehow noticed the awkward nerdy girl with too many flashcards and not enough confidence—and I think:

Maybe this is the start of everything.

And as I walk into my dorm, his hand warm in mine, I'm not even nervous anymore.

Just hopeful.

Just in love.

Just his.

I sit on the edge of the bed, picking up my phone in an effort to distract myself. I shoot Aubrey a quick text message reply and then open my email.

One new message from Kat greets me.

I'm filled with dread—but then I think of Jack's accusations. The truth is I like the life I'm creating, one where I focus less on the ways he doesn't fulfill me and more on the things I can do for myself that will. I open Kat's email and read the brief message.

> You have a date tonight. 9:30pm. 732 Amsterdam.
> See attached photos.

I groan as I open the two photos. The file name of the first reads "Julie." Tears instantly well in my eyes when a young woman's face pops up. She's in the hospital, her face beaten and bruised, the swelling so severe she's unrecognizable. Whoever did this to her deserves to pay. Deserves to feel the pain this woman must have felt. Her lip is split and bleeding; bandages cover one side of her head, her cheek is sewn together with stitches, and one eye is swollen shut. She'd probably require plastic surgery to fix what this man did to her. I close that photo and open the next.

My heart nearly stops.

It's a man in a suit, thinning hair slicked back like a businessman's, his smirk already making my skin crawl. And what's worse: I know this man. His face is familiar, but I can't place it. I search the photo for any details; the only one is a sign hanging in the background that says ASSOCIATION OF NORTHEAST SURGEONS GALA. I move to my internet search window and type in the name of the event. The first result that pops up is the website for the gala, and at the top of the website is the same photo of the man who's apparently my next target. The caption reads "Guest Speaker William H. Terry, Surgeon General of the United States."

I close the browser window and shut my laptop. The gravity of this moment hits me like a bag of bricks. This man is powerful, appointed by the president, and I'm supposed to go on a date with him, lure him into hurting me, and then gather enough evidence to ruin his career? For the first time I think that this isn't just a game—this is high stakes, something that could ruin me . . . Spending time with powerful people like this could even be the end of me.

Everything in me wants to believe that this isn't real, that whatever muddy situation I've found myself in is harmless, just a matter of exacting justice on pathetic little men . . . but this man isn't little. He's accomplished, he's in the public eye, he has powerful friends—and for the first time I feel actual fear. I open my laptop again, composing a reply to Kat and The Society.

> I'm sorry, I can't.

Kat's reply arrives before I can even close my browser window and forget this ever happened.

> You must. You're her only hope. She lives on disability now and the report she filed against him was "lost." Wear the dress that's being delivered to you. It's red—his favorite color—he'll find you.

My heart sinks as I realize what this is.
He thinks he's hired a hooker for tonight.
And I'm it.

SEVENTEEN

Ellie

The red dress itches.

It's too tight in the chest, too short to sit in without tugging, too bright for a place like this. But that's the point, isn't it? To stand out. To lure. I sit in the corner booth of a dive bar on Amsterdam, surrounded by flickering neon signs and the stale stench of spilled beer and old secrets. The vinyl beneath me sticks to the backs of my thighs. I cross and uncross my legs, pretending I belong here, pretending this is just another night.

Then he walks in.

The Surgeon General.

He's exactly what I expected and somehow worse—slicked-back hair with too much gel, a cheap suit trying to look expensive, and the kind of smug smile that makes your skin crawl. He's scanning the room like he's already claimed everything in it, and when his eyes land on me, I feel it in my spine.

"You here for me?" he says as he slides into the booth without asking. His voice is smooth like oil—thick, slick, dangerous.

I smile. Just a little. "Sure am."

He doesn't look convinced, but he doesn't care. He flags the waitress with a lazy wave. "Whiskey. Neat." Then to me, "What do you want?"

"Soda."

That makes him laugh. Loud, grating. "A sober one, huh? That's unusual. What's your name, sweetheart?"

I stare at him, unblinking. He thinks I'm playing a part. That's fine. Let him. "Julie."

"Sweet. I like that. You from the city?" he asks, leaning in, elbows on the sticky table. He smells like old sweat and too much aftershave.

"No." I slide my black cardigan off. His eyes roam up and down my form with interest.

"Didn't think so. You've got that lost-little-girl thing. Shame, really. Never lasts long in this business."

His hand moves under the table, bold and slow, landing on my thigh like it has a right to be there. I don't flinch. I reach down and remove it, calm as anything, like swatting a fly.

He laughs again, but there's something sharp under it now. "Seriously? Most prudish hooker they've ever sent me."

I tilt my head, forcing a smile. "They?"

"Yeah, your boss. Handler. *Pimp*. Whatever the hell you call him." He lifts his glass, downs the whiskey in one swallow. "He promised me something *special*. Said you were new. Said you were good."

The words curdle in my stomach.

"How many girls have there been before me?" I ask quietly, mostly to myself. He doesn't hear the threat under my voice. He hears an opportunity.

"Enough to know what I like. And what I don't." He reaches into his pocket, pulls out his phone. "Want me to call him? Tell him his girl's not performing? Get you replaced with someone who knows how to do the damn job?"

He still thinks I'm something he purchased. Something disposable. But beneath my fear, there's something else rising—something molten and ancient and cold at the same time.

Who does he think I work for?

He slurs something about how girls these days have no respect, no gratitude, no spine. He's not even looking at me now—just talking, rambling, proud of himself.

And I'm watching him like a scientist studies a specimen.

"I've got a room upstairs," he says suddenly, slamming the empty glass on the table. "Come on, sweetheart. Don't make me drag you."

My stomach flips. My skin crawls. Every nerve in my body screams for me to run.

But I don't move. I breathe. I stand slowly, the dress riding high as I slide out of the booth. He grabs at my waist like I'm already his, and I let him—for a moment.

Just long enough.

Let him think I'm weak. Let him think I'm scared.

Let him think I'm just another name in his phone, just another body he gets to ruin and forget.

He doesn't know.

He has no idea who I really am.

And he'll never see what's coming.

I follow him through a shabby door behind the bar and up the stairs, each creaking step a countdown. The hallway smells like mildew and cheap floor polish. His cologne hangs in the air like a chokehold, musky and arrogant, clouding my lungs. He's muttering something about how "this better be worth it," and I pretend to be too nervous to talk. I guess I am.

The room is exactly what I expected—stained rug, sagging twin bed, one dim lamp casting long shadows across the walls like watching eyes. He shuts the door with a flick of his wrist and turns to me, that smarmy smile curling across his face.

"C'mere, sweetheart," he slurs, reaching for my waist again.

I let him. Let him pull me close and mash his mouth against mine. His lips are wet, forceful, and taste like whiskey and rot. I kiss him back with all the tenderness of a corpse, letting him paw at my hips, my breasts, my ass. His hands are everywhere, greedy and uncoordinated. My stomach coils tighter with every touch.

I pull away just enough to breathe and flash him a coy smile. "You want me to be good, don't you?"

"Damn right," he pants, stumbling backward toward the bed. "Get on your knees and suck me off."

I take a step closer, eyes wide, voice light. "Not yet. Let's have a little fun first."

He flops onto the bed with a grunt, spreading his legs like he's king of the world. His fly is already halfway down. I crawl onto the mattress slowly, straddling him with practiced grace, dragging my fingers down his chest as my heartbeat hammers in my ears.

"Tease," he groans, eyelids fluttering as I start undoing the buttons on his shirt. One. Two. Three. My hands tremble, not from nerves, but from the force it takes not to drive my knuckles into his throat.

"You like slow, don't you?" I whisper, licking the sweat from his collarbone. He grunts approval.

He's drunk enough not to notice when I slide his sleeves down just to his elbows, not fully off his arms, then tie the wrists around the bed's iron headboard. I knot them together gently, playfully, like a game. He's at my mercy now.

"Whoa, now"—he chuckles—"getting kinky, huh?"

I giggle, soft and breathy. "Don't move."

He won't. Not yet. He thinks this is foreplay.

I kiss my way down his stomach, the flesh loose and greasy beneath my mouth. I can feel the bile rising in my throat, but I push it down. I only think of *Julie*. The real Julie. It probably wasn't even her real name. I don't need to know her name to know what he did to her, though.

His pants are around his ankles now. He moans, his head lolling back. "That's it, baby. That's what I—"

He doesn't finish.

Because when I rise up, it's not with my mouth.

It's with the knife.

Small, sharp, the same matte black as my bootheel, and sheathed in a small leather case to avoid cutting my skin. I'd tucked it in at the last moment before I left my apartment. My fingers curl around the hilt, my heart as cold as steel.

He blinks, confused. "Wha—?"

I straddle his chest, lean in so close I can smell the panic starting to seep through his sweat. I smile.

"This one's for Julie," I whisper.

And I start to carve.

He screams the moment the blade bites into skin. I shove a balled-up corner of the dingy blanket into his mouth to stifle the noise. I drag the knife slow, deliberate, from his collarbone down to the start of his gut. The J is messy. He's thrashing. The U gets cleaner. By the L, I'm soaked in blood. I work through his cries, through the begging moans, the muffled shrieks that bounce off the walls and seem to crawl back into him.

Julie. In thick, screaming red.

He bucks, trying to break free, but the shirt sleeves hold. His face is mottled, panicked, soaked with tears now. Good.

I lean in again, voice calm. "May you never forget."

Then I bite.

His earlobe splits between my teeth, and I feel his blood gush hot down my chin. He screams harder.

I wipe the blade on his chest and slip it back into my boot. I climb off, straighten my dress, sticky and soaked now with his blood. The red fabric hides the truth beautifully, but I slide my black cardigan over my shoulders anyway.

I don't look back.

I walk downstairs slowly, each step measured. In the bar no one glances at me. No one notices.

I push open the front door and step out into the night.

Amsterdam Avenue hums with taxis, sirens, and drunken laughter.

My dress clings to me, wet and dark.

The perfect camouflage.

Crimson justice. And no one the wiser.

My cell buzzes with an incoming text message then. I fish it out of my clutch and find another message from an anonymous number.

I wonder how your husband would feel if he knew the truth.

EIGHTEEN

Ellie

I don't check my email for the next three days. I don't dare. I've avoided the newspaper headlines, avoided Aubrey, and even Jack—which hasn't been hard because he's been escaping to work since our last fight. I've done my best to cover my tracks—disposing of the knife I used to slice up the Surgeon General in a dumpster off of 73rd on my walk home and washing the little red dress soaked in blood three times. I don't know how to cover up a crime, but I did what I could.

Truth be told, I'm afraid to check my email for a few reasons: One, because I don't want to know what happened after I left that bar, and two, because I'm afraid of my next target—afraid because there are never any instructions on how to deal with these encounters. I'm left to my own devices, and maybe carving up the Surgeon General went too far. But I didn't kill him. I just left him with scars that will last a lifetime. I'm particularly pleased with the fact that if these men try to report me, there will be mutually assured destruction. The Surgeon General can't report me without risking authorities uncovering his own illicit activities, and the resulting public scandal that could cost him his job.

Now, three mornings later, I'm feeling restless. I'm supposed to go to work this morning, but I've already emailed and taken the day off. My anxiety has hit new levels, and engaging in the mundane, crunching numbers and pretending to be poised, sounds unbearable. Plus, I can't handle the watercooler conversations about the Surgeon General if it hits the headlines. So instead, I've perched myself on the sofa with Netflix and ice cream, healing from the horror I inflicted on one of America's most prestigious appointed officials.

Part of me wants to tell everything to Aubrey. I want to hear her tell me that it's worth it—that what I'm doing is justified—but I'm just not sure anymore. I'm so lost in my new position with The Society that I can't see right from wrong.

The door to the apartment opens then, and Jack interrupts my thoughts. "Hey—still not feeling well?"

I brace myself for his scrutiny, keeping my words short. "Still under the weather."

"Heard there's a bug going around—I'll have to keep my distance from you, Typhoid Mary," he says.

I don't laugh. He has no idea.

"I was just about to get some work done from home." I stand, heading in the direction of the bedroom.

"Hey—wait—funny question." He sets his laptop bag down on the dining room table. "Did you hear about that scandal with the Columbia professor?"

I push a hand over my head and sigh. "The *New York Post* article? Yeah, I saw that."

"Did you know him?" Jack crosses his arms, leaning against the kitchen island as he watches me.

"No," I reply. "He was in the law department, right? I never went to that side of campus."

Jack nods. "Huh."

"Did you know him?" I turn the question on my husband.

"I think I had him for a lecture once—seemed like a good guy." Jack busies himself with something in his laptop bag.

"Did you forget some files here?"

"Stopped by for a shower and change of clothes. This Allegiance case has me burning the candle at both ends."

I nod, unwilling to say more. Normally I would ask how he's been lately—I'd be the soft, nurturing wife he's used to—but I don't have it in me. Not anymore. It occurs to me then that I've been overextending myself and showing up for this man as my best representation of the picture-perfect wife, and why? Jack hasn't shown up for me like the doting, protective husband I would expect. Not now, maybe not ever. Why should I be expected to give 100 percent when he doesn't even show up 50 percent of the time? Not physically and certainly not emotionally. In truth, I've been living like a single woman for a long time, in bed with pajamas and takeout by eight p.m. most nights while he does God knows what all week long.

"Since you're home, do you wanna get some lunch, maybe?" he asks.

I pause on my way to the bedroom, letting my hardened gaze linger a few extra beats. "I'm not feeling well."

"Oh, right." A frown flickers across his face. "Let me know if you change your mind—"

"I won't." A chill threads through my words.

He doesn't say anything else. I walk to the bedroom, letting the door close quietly behind me. Looking for a distraction from our strained interaction, I open my laptop and navigate to my email. I've been afraid to check my inbox the last few days, fearing a new assignment from Kat, but I can't avoid it forever.

The only new message that isn't spam is from The Society. The timestamp is late last night. I open it as feelings of dread swirl in my stomach.

> Friday. 9 Doyers Street. 8pm. Corner booth. Further details to follow.

My heart hammers as I plug the location into an internet search bar and find that it's an exclusive cocktail bar named Apotheke in Chinatown. And just like that, I have my next assignment. I close my email and sigh. I'm not sure how long I can keep up this juggling act of a double life with Jack. I shove that thought to the back of my mind, though, thinking that he spends most of his nights away from home, wining and dining clients at restaurants and bars around Manhattan or poring over case files fifty city blocks from our bed.

I blink away tears as I think about how dull and domesticated my life with Jack has become, like we're living in a constant state of barely tolerating each other. Is this all that's left of us? A future that looks like the past, no new adventures, only loneliness and farewells and death to look forward to? We're together and maybe that's all there is. Maybe that's enough. But something unsettled rattles inside of me.

But what if it's not?

NINETEEN

Ellie

"This is swanky," Aubrey says as we enter Apotheke on Friday night.

The server greets us and asks if we have a reservation. I nod and mumble my name. She smiles politely and then guides us to a small two-top table in the center of the room. Rich green velvet sofas line the walls and a golden art deco–style bar anchors one side of the room. We both settle on the couch and face outward so we can watch the front door and the bar simultaneously.

"That dress was made for you," Aubrey says. "I wish invites and fabulous designer party dresses appeared on *my* doorstep. You've really found yourself in some sort of twilight zone, and I'd do anything to catch a ride on that train."

"The built-in corset in this dress makes me feel like I can't breathe," I complain.

"But you look like a million bucks." She bumps shoulders with me.

"Thanks," I reply, glancing down at the cocktail menu.

"So where did you tell your husband you're at tonight?" she asks.

"I didn't," I say, my tone clipped as I think about him. "We got in a fight a few mornings ago and haven't spoken since. We're like strangers. I'd say it's unbearable but . . . I kind of like it. The pressure of maintaining a relationship feels . . . less."

"Maybe space is just what you needed," she says with a shrug, then smiles when the server reaches us and begins explaining the mixologist's cocktail of the day: bourbon, maple syrup, hints of walnut, cardamom, and bitters, all smoked tableside. I order one just to see what the fuss is about, and Aubrey asks for a gin and tonic. The server leaves with our orders and Aubrey turns to me, about to say something, before her mouth rounds in an O and her eyes widen. "I bet that's him. Look at the way he commands a room."

I turn to the door, and I freeze.

I swallow my shock, then shift deeper into the shadows of the bar. "I hope not."

"Why?" she whispers.

I allow my hair to cascade over one side of my face to remain out of sight. "Because that's my dad."

"What?" Her voice raises a few octaves. "Really?"

"Really," I say.

"Fuck, well how's that for a surprise," she says, eyes riveted on my father's broad form crossing the small space. "Shit, El," she says under her breath, "they've seated him at the corner table. Just like the email said."

My heartbeat roars in my ears like a freight train as the implications of this settle in. Could my father really be my next target? "This must be a mistake."

"You think?" Aubrey watches as my dad settles himself on the luxe velvet cushions and then nods to the server. "He seems like a regular here, El."

"No—this can't be right." I shake my head, unwilling to look in his direction.

"Did Kat give you any more details about this target?"

I blink away my pain and confusion as I think back on the note that arrived last night with the designer corseted dress I'm now wearing. "It said . . . he's a wealthy real estate man who's abused dozens of women for decades."

"Do you think—"

"No," I cut her off. "I don't think it's him. It can't be. There's no way. That would mean he's been living a double life—"

"Like you have been?" she interjects.

I groan. The urge to stand and stomp out of this swanky cocktail bar is strong. "How can this be right?"

"You said he was a workaholic—it's easy to keep secrets when you're never home."

"Yeah, but—"

"Makes you wonder what other secrets the people in your life are keeping, right?" She smiles and thanks the server when our drinks arrive. The server makes a show of lighting my bourbon on fire before covering it with a glass dome and telling us it will smoke for the next five minutes and impart layers of flavor to the drink. I'm thankful for the clouds of smoke that linger at our table, twisting and spiraling just like the thoughts in my mind.

If it's true, if my father is my next target . . . surely Kat knew. The Society was clear about the research they do for each new recruit to their group. They knew everything about me: my real name, my place of employment, my education . . .

"I don't understand what they expect from me," I finally admit, nearly choking on the frustration that's forming in my throat. "Do they really expect me to target my father? Ruin his reputation? Aubrey . . ." I glance at my friend. "Maybe I was wrong about the professor. If The Society got this one wrong, what else are they wrong about? What if the rape with the professor and Savannah didn't happen? What if I ruined the life and reputation of a man who was innocent?"

Aubrey raises her eyebrows. "Or maybe they're right, El. He tried to rape you too. That professor was an asshole—you could see it in the arrogant sparkle in his eye."

I swallow, my anxiety rising. "But . . . if they're right, then this changes . . . *everything*. My entire world, what I thought I knew, what I've been told—what's real, what's not . . ."

She looks pensive as she sips her gin and tonic.

"Wait—do you think . . . ?" She trails off without finishing her question.

"What?" I breathe, afraid of her answer.

She chews on her bottom lip, eyes warming with sympathy.

And then a flash of awareness courses through me. I know what she's thinking. I wish I didn't. She's wondering the same thing I am.

Is this why I was chosen by The Society?

Because of my access to one of the most powerful businessmen in the city? I blink, my vision tunneling to the smoke that's trapped under the glass dome between us. For the first time in my life I feel caught in a trap that won't let go, and I have no idea where to turn.

I wasn't invited into The Society because of my father's status.

I was invited because of his *crimes*.

TWENTY

Aubrey

"I know, I know. I tried to tell her," I say into the phone, frustration climbing in my tone. I wait a long moment for a reply that never comes. "Okay—well, I have shit to do. I should go."

"Don't forget Saturday," comes the order through the speaker.

"I'll be there," I retort, then hang up. I drop my bag on the table by the door and then kick the heels off my feet. I think of the shock on Ellie's face tonight when she realized that The Society has set her up to take down her father. What a tough pill to swallow—poor girl.

It took us less than twenty minutes to finish our drinks before we left Apotheke, unnoticed by her father, and hit up the dive bar a few blocks away. We split a bottle of cheap champagne between us as she considered her next move. Ignore the directive from Kat and The Society? Pretend it never happened and move on with her life? Confront her father? All seem impossible—once you know something like that you can't go back. I feel for the girl, but not so much that it distracts me from my own purpose. I can't let useless emotions like empathy get in the way of the greater good, and even if Ellie doesn't see it now, my way is the best way. She'll get there—I have faith in that. I'm so close to driving the final wedge between her life *before* and the one that will come *after*. I just need a little more time to set things in motion, a little more time to make her see the truth. An idea occurs to me then, and I send a quick email to an old friend who works on the police force. The reply comes minutes later with a pdf file attached—it's all the information I need.

I'm still awake reading through the file an hour later when Ellie's text message comes.

I can't sleep. Up for a nightcap?

Sure, I reply instantly. It's after one in the morning but I haven't gotten much sleep since I moved into this building, so I don't mind. I'm tapping on her door a few minutes later in pajamas, a bottle of red wine in hand.

"Long time, no see, stranger." I wink when Ellie opens the door.

A faint smile crosses her face before it's gone again. "Hi. I can't sleep. I had a nightmare."

"Oh, shit. I'm sorry," I say as I walk in. "What about?"

Ellie remains silent as I follow her into the kitchen and she takes down two wine glasses. "My mom."

"Oh." I can't hide the shock in my voice.

"I woke up in a cold sweat with what I think is her voice in my head screaming, *find me, find me*. It's awful."

"Do you dream about her a lot?" I ask, as we settle on the couch that overlooks the windows and Columbus Circle.

"Too much, especially considering I have no memories of her. She's been dead for so long. I feel like my brain is torturing me," she admits, then sips her wine.

"Brains suck like that," I offer. "I'm glad you called me; I'm always up for a nightcap. I can empathize with the mom stuff—even before my mom passed we weren't really on the best terms. I lived a long time without her in my life, by choice. I wished her all the best but she was dead to me long before she actually died, you know? I think I mourned the mother I never had when she passed away, not her *actual* passing, if that makes sense. Family is so complicated sometimes."

"Yeah, add to that a sprinkle of mental illness and the train really goes off the tracks." Ellie's laugh is wry.

"No doubt," I say. "I don't know if this is the right time . . . actually, I don't think there's ever a right time for this. But I reached out to a friend on the police force—we used to date; he's my ex-boyfriend and he owes me a solid after he did me dirty when we broke up. So I had him run some searches on your dad, and, El—he found some records that were supposed to be sealed. It's not good." I unfold the few dozen sheets of paper I printed out before coming over—the most damning reports—and toss them on the coffee table in front of us. "We might need another bottle of wine for this."

Ellie sucks in a heavy breath before picking up the freshly printed paperwork.

"I hope you're not mad—" I say.

"No, of course not. I appreciate it," she replies, but I can hear the dread in her voice. It is what it is, I think. She needs to know what she's dealing with—that everything she thought she knew has been a falsely constructed narrative meant to hide the truth from her. She glances down at the first sheet of paper. "Oh God," Ellie says. "I think I'm going to throw up."

Bullseye, I think. But what I say is, "I'm sorry. It's so awful I didn't know if I should share it with you."

"No, no, I need this." She flips to the second sheet and scans it before flipping the papers over and setting them back on the coffee table. "He raped someone."

I can almost see her heart hammering in her throat.

"There's more," I continue, determined to give her the full picture even if it kills her. "There's a cancelled order for child support."

"W-what? What does that mean?"

"It means he had a baby with the woman he raped—one of them at least. The charges for lapsed support were dropped, though, so I bet he settled with her out of court," I explain.

"Oh." I can see goose bumps rise on Ellie's arms.

"I searched the woman's name—there isn't anything on the internet about the case itself, but I did find her social media profiles. She has a pretty unique name, so I'm pretty confident it's her."

"Oh." Ellie's voice is barely above a whisper.

"She lives on Long Island now." I push. "She owns a hair salon."

Ellie only nods, finally at a loss for words.

"El," I say with a sigh, pretending this is harder for me than it actually is, "she has a daughter."

Ellie blinks, then nods.

"And she's the right age to be"—I pause for dramatic effect—"your half sister."

"Fuck..." Tears well in Ellie's eyes then. "You were right," she says, wiping at her tears. "There isn't enough wine on the island of Manhattan to get me through this."

I frown, feigning as much sympathy as I can before I pull her in for a tight hug.

"Do you know her name? My half sister, I mean."

I nod. "I made a note of it in the margins of the last page." I rub Ellie's back with as much care as I can muster. "I'm sorry your father isn't who he says he is, and I hate that I was the bearer of bad news."

"It's okay—it honestly makes more sense now. I was thinking I would just ignore any more emails from The Society but... I don't think I can now. It seems like they hold the key to a piece of my past that I didn't know existed."

"Yeah . . ." I say, nodding. "And I hate to say it, but there's more in his record, Ellie. I bet he paid a lot of people off to keep this part of his past quiet. And this is just reports from the women who went to the police—I'm sure there's more who were too afraid to report him . . ."

"Yeah . . ." Ellie presses her lips together, eyes lingering on the stack of papers. "I think I need some time alone. I think I'm going to take a sleeping pill and just knock myself out 'til next week. I'm sorry I called you so late." Ellie stands, walking in the direction of the door. I'm guessing that's my cue to leave. "Thanks for being such a good friend."

"Yeah, of course. I'm always here for you, anytime." I wrap her in a final hug and then excuse myself and walk back down the hall to my apartment, my grin growing a little wider with every step. *Ready. Aim. Fire.*

TWENTY-ONE

Ellie

I type the name of my father's daughter into the search bar. *Dakota Lily Wilder.* My heart pounds in my chest as a list of social media profiles pop up. The only one that mentions that name exactly is at the top. I lean in, squint, then click on her name. Does she look like me? I can't tell. Her hair is an unnaturally bleached shade of platinum blond. Her cheekbones are high, and her piercing ice-blue eyes are lined with a thick ring of kohl liner. I don't recognize anything in her features, but then, that probably doesn't mean much. She looks to be within a few years of my own age, though the dark circles under her eyes indicate an overall sense of exhaustion.

Her profile is set to private, so the only thing I have to go off of is the few profile pictures that are available to me.

"You still up?" Jack's voice pulls me from my thoughts. I close my browser window and then shut my laptop before turning just as he opens the door to the bedroom. "Saw the light on from the sidewalk when I walked up."

"Can't sleep—you know how it goes," I murmur.

"Hey"—he steps further into the room—"I wanted to touch base with you about the other day."

I suppress a groan. I hate that he always addresses me like one of his clients—careful, detached. I don't have the mental capacity to navigate this on top of everything else going on today.

When I don't respond, he continues, "Well, I was thinking about how much we've been through and that it's probably not fair for me to hold you to such a high standard when it comes to mental health stuff—"

"What?" I say, shocked.

"Yeah—you know what I mean. I was talking to your dad about some stuff with your mom, and it made me realize—"

"You were talking to my dad about our fight?" I interrupt.

"Yeah, I mean, it came up—"

"So . . . that's it? I don't even get a proper sorry then?"

"No . . . is that what you expected?" His brows crinkle with confusion, as if the concept of saying sorry isn't even in his wheelhouse. Actually, the more I think about it . . . Jack *never* says sorry. Not once that I can recall in the ten years since we met.

"I mean—yes. I did expect a sorry at some point." I get up off the bed, cross my arms, and face him fully.

"I don't really think an apology is warranted—Jesus, Ellie. You keep me up day and night worrying about if you're taking care of yourself or . . . hell, if you're even safe to be left alone." He grasps my wrist, pulls out my arm, and gestures to the faded bruises marring my skin.

I yank my arm back, clenching and unclenching my fists. "I can't believe you came home to tell me this bullshit."

"It's a good fucking thing I did because here you are with an empty bottle of wine and pulling another all-nighter. What are you doing anyway? Having another *emotional* affair with some loser on the internet? Finding more ways to piss me off? I know we're both busy with work, but you could put in a little more effort to support me since I'm the one who carries the financial burden in this marriage."

I grit my teeth, working my jaw back and forth. I choke back tears because I do not want this man to know that he's getting under my skin. Not when he'll only use it for emotional blackmail later.

"You know, I've even been wondering if you've been experiencing the early signs of a psychotic break." His eyes bore into mine. I blink, swallow the anger down, then try to catch one of the raging thoughts moving through my head.

"Are you fucking kidding me?" I seethe. Blood-red rage tunnels my vision. I can't catch a single thought or form a word to express how I'm feeling at this moment.

"You should go," I finally murmur, sliding back into bed and tucking myself into the sheets. I turn over, facing away from the man I vowed to share the rest of my life with.

"Go? Are you fucking kidding? I pay the rent on this fucking apartment you just *had* to have."

I don't answer him. I may never answer him again. Expressing thoughts and feelings to Jack Taylor is a waste of time.

"Fine. Just wanted to let you know I won't be home tomorrow. I have to go to the Jersey office for a few days." He pauses, waiting for my reply. It doesn't come. "I'll sleep in the guest bedroom tonight."

I still don't reply as I fight the stray tears leaking from my eyes. The only thought running through my mind: *How did we get here?*

TWENTY-TWO

Ellie

Sweat drips from my skin as I plant my hands on the brick wall and wail. My anguish cuts through the silence, terror, and frustration filling me.

"I'm watching you. It will all be over soon." A thready voice shushes me.

I don't know where I am, only that I'm trapped.

"Help." I moan, thrashing, then realize that my wrists are bound. *"Help me, please."*

A nurse opens the door of my room and then an alarm echoes through my ears. I wake with a jolt, sticky with sweat, my muscles tense and aching from the unnatural position I've been sleeping in. I gasp for breath, my heart racing as I push myself out of bed. The door alarm sounds again, the piercing shriek rattling my bones.

"Ugh." I push a hand through my damp hair and glance at the clock on the nightstand. "Holy shit." The time reads 4:30 p.m., in neon blue. I suck in another breath and then stand, moving across the room to open the curtains. Sunshine bathes the bedroom in light and makes my eyes burn. I move in the direction of the bathroom and flip on the light; the first thing I notice is fresh bruises at my wrists. "Oh God."

I slip my thumb along the shades of bright blue and purple, flashes of my nightmare coming back to me. My wrists bound together, my pained screams echoing around the small room. Locked in an asylum, left to rot. Just like Mom. *How's that for a family legacy?*

I push down a ball of emotion and then splash cold water on my face. My reflection, tired and drawn, stares back at me. I'm starting to look older than my thirty-three years, and the lack of sleep makes me *feel* older. I really should take some time off for a spa getaway. Or maybe I should just move out. The thought lingers in my mind unbidden. I never considered leaving my husband, but last night changed things. I can't quite place my finger on *why* exactly, but suddenly my perspective shifted. Everything I thought I knew was turned on its head, as if a fog had cleared in the span of a single moment and I could see my husband for who he truly is.

I shake the thoughts from my mind and leave my bedroom, heading for the front door. When I open it, I find a food delivery. Not the takeout type, but a box of groceries. I wonder if maybe this is Jack's way of apologizing. I bring the box in the house and set it on the kitchen counter. I pull out small glass bottles of milk, cream, and local honey. That's it. Why would Jack order such a random arrangement of items? I empty the box and find a small notecard in the bottom that says:

Check your email.

My heartbeat ticks up a few notches. I put the milk and cream in the fridge and then lean against the counter as I open the email app on my phone and refresh my inbox. There it is, another email from The Society.

Dread freezes me. This is it. This is where I find out exactly what they want from me, and what it has to do with my dad.

> Special farm-to-table delivery for your next target. Leave the honey and cream at the office for his afternoon tea and the milk in his fridge at home. You're the only one he trusts. Dozens of women are counting on you. Don't disappoint us.

Angry tears fill my eyes as I hit delete on the message and close my email. All I keep thinking is, *What's in that fucking milk?* I think back on the cows and bees surrounding the estate in Westchester the weekend I visited. Maybe it's just that—maybe it's just fresh milk and locally sourced honey... or maybe it's not. No, it's *definitely* not. I think back on the email. *You're the only one he trusts.* My stomach turns in painful cartwheels. I just found out my father isn't who he says he is, and now I'm expected to act out some sort of revenge? On the only man who was there for me? The man who raised me and kept me safe and ... *fathered another child?* I swallow down the painful realization before I set my phone down and head back into my bedroom. I need to get out of this apartment—I feel like I'm going stir-crazy. In twenty-four hours, my entire world has turned upside down. I want to jump in an Uber and go to Westchester and demand answers, but at the same time I want to head in the opposite direction and never look back. I want to forget the last twenty-four hours even happened. But how could I ever? I have a life here. My father is my boss—my father is my husband's boss. I think how deep the implications of this run.

I wander to my walk-in closet and find my favorite outfit, a knee-length floral summer dress. It's simple, breezy, and makes me feel like I'm about to sip cocktails on the beach in Montauk. Jack always compliments me when I wear it, so I wear it a lot in the summer. Fifteen minutes later I've added a little blush to my cheeks and slipped on a pair of simple flats and am walking the half dozen blocks to the Peninsula Hotel. It has a spectacular rooftop view of 5th Avenue, especially after dark, and it's the place where Jack and I had one of our first dates. It's always been nostalgic for me, and I've been meaning to ask him if he wants to go since we haven't been there in a long time, but we've been so very *off* lately.

I reach the rooftop in fifteen minutes and am settling myself at a quiet corner of the bar when I see him.

Jack.

He's probably here for a client meeting. But . . . didn't he say he was spending the night in Jersey? Maybe his plans fell through or a client cancelled. His face looks drawn and exhausted, like a man who slept on the couch last night. A pang of guilt shoots through me for adding stress to his life. On some level he's right—he does work hard, and maybe I should be more aware of that. I decide to walk over to him, if only just to offer him a quick hug, but then I see her.

She walks around the corner, her eyes trained squarely on my husband. I choke on anxiety as it registers that she looks like she's on a date—slinky red dress and dark red lips. She looks beautiful, and every part the woman I am not. Elegant, poised, polished, *stunning.* Her kohl-lined eyes scan the room and her gaze catches mine. I am chilled to the bone. Her smile falters, and then she seems to change course and aim directly for me.

She pauses in front of me. "El—crazy seeing you here."

"Hi, Aubrey."

"What brings you here?" she asks.

The bartender hovers to take my order but I wave him off, asking for a moment longer. "Just thought I'd take myself out for a date. You?"

"I'm meeting an old friend," is all she says, eyes scanning the bar as if she's looking for someone. "It doesn't look like they're here yet, though."

I glance over her shoulder to see that my husband is sitting by himself, looking anywhere but over here.

"Hey—I was gonna ask if you wanted to grab lunch with me tomorrow afternoon," she says. "There's this new noodle bar near Lincoln Center I've been wanting to check out."

"Yeah—ugh—I'd love to but I have to go over some reports for a big client before Monday, so I'd hate to commit and then cancel."

"Okay—well, just let me know. I could always bring you takeout too—"

"Thanks, you're sweet." I give her a forced smile. "I'll let you know."

"Okay." Her eyes linger a few silent beats on mine before she smiles with a smile that doesn't reach her eyes. "Well, I'll leave you alone. Text me later."

"Sure," I shoot back, shifting my gaze to the bartender just to have anything other than her to look at. She turns, crossing the length of the bar before settling at the opposite end, nearest to my husband. She shifts awkwardly on the barstool, eyes cast down to a cocktail menu in front of her.

The bartender returns to me then, and I shake my head. "I'm not feeling well after all—I think I'm going to skip a drink. Thank you, though."

I stand, gathering my bag and attempting to control my rioting emotions before turning to walk back down the hall to the elevators. I punch the down arrow, and the doors slide open silently. I step inside, thankful to finally be alone. As the doors close, stubborn tears begin a slow slide down my cheeks as one thought runs on repeat in my mind.

Is Aubrey having an affair with my husband?

TWENTY-THREE

Ellie

As soon as I walk into the apartment I find my laptop and open an internet search engine. I type in "psychosis" and then "schizophrenia" and spend the next twenty minutes reading about the different symptoms of the disorders. I keep hearing Jack's accusation in my mind: *You've been experiencing the early signs of a psychotic break.* I don't think I am, not based on the internet's diagnosis anyway, but the disorders have a spectrum of symptoms and a few of them match: difficulty sleeping, obviously, but also paranoia, mood swings, and withdrawing from social situations. I think of mentioning it to my therapist, but I've cancelled the last few appointments because I've been so busy, and she took me off her schedule, so I'm not even sure when I'll see her again.

Then I type in the name of the facility my mother was admitted to and the year she died. I was only seven and don't know many details—by the time I was old enough to ask questions, my father had moved on and never seemed to want to discuss it. He often said that thinking about it was like rubbing salt in the wound, so he preferred to keep his head down and stay firmly rooted in the present.

I scroll through the first few pages of results but I don't find anything interesting. I move to the news tab in my browser window then, and I find an article about a nurse's strike that happened in the month leading up to my mother's death. The writer interviewed one nurse in particular, Rachel Franklin. The interview is accompanied by a photo of a small group of nurses holding signs outside the facility. While the other nurses standing with her are older, Rachel is young, probably fresh out of nursing school, and she still might be alive. It's been over twenty-five years since then, so she's probably around fifty now.

I open a new search window and type in her name along with the name of the facility. A LinkedIn page is the first result, followed by one of her social media profiles. I click on both and confirm that it does seem to be the same woman. I spend a few minutes lingering on her social media profile page—a photo of her sipping a cocktail on a warm beach somewhere stares back at me. Before I can think twice, I click *add friend* and then wait patiently to see what happens.

I don't have to wait long. Rachel Franklin confirms my request a few minutes later. It's funny how this woman doesn't even know me, but she's so quick to accept me into her life.

I jump over to the *message* button and then begin typing.

Hi, I know you don't know me but my mother was admitted to Greystone Park Psychiatric when I was a little girl. I never saw her again. She died there and I've never known exactly what happened to her. I think you might have been working there when she was admitted, would you be willing to talk to me? I've always had a few questions.

I wait a few long moments and then am surprised to see three blinking dots pop up on the message screen that indicate that Rachel is replying.

I swallow the anxiety lodged in my throat when a message pops up.

Sure!

An alert rattles to life on my phone then. I'm receiving a call from Rachel via the messaging app. *Holy shit.*

I answer on the first ring.

"Hi! I thought it would be easier to call—so many weird things happened that year. It was my first job out of nursing school, and let's just say that working at a psychiatric facility was *not* what I expected."

"I bet," I reply. "Thanks for being willing to talk to me."

"Of course!" Her tone is bubbly, helpful. "What was your mom's name?"

"Valeria Thomas."

"Hm, beautiful name but I don't remember her. What was she admitted for? I handled a lot of the new intakes and worked in the records department most days. They don't trust the newbies with the really insane cases."

I nearly falter when she says *insane*. "She was having hallucinations . . . she . . . tried to burn down our house. *With me in it.*"

"Oh," comes her reply. The line remains silent for a few long beats. "I'm afraid I don't remember her, but let me call a friend. She worked there for twenty years—she's older now, but we still meet for lunch every few months. She has a good memory for this stuff and a lot of great stories from back then. We get together and just talk and talk about those days. She saw *a lot*. I'll give her a call and then call you back if she remembers anything; is that okay?"

"Yeah, that would be great. Thank you so much."

"Sure, honey." And just like that the line goes dead.

I sit down on a barstool, my mind falling back to Aubrey's red lips and Jack's drawn face. They had to have been meeting each other there, right? There's no way the three of us were all there by coincidence, like some twisted little love triangle. My heart cleaves in my chest as I think about an affair happening between them right under my nose. When would they have met? Is that why Aubrey moved into the apartment down the hallway? And why would they do this to me?

By the time Rachel calls me back thirty minutes later, I've come to the conclusion that the run-in at the Peninsula tonight really was some weird coincidence. It is an iconic place, popular with businessmen, and it's only a quick walk from Columbus Circle.

"My friend remembers something interesting," Rachel says, as soon as I've picked up the phone.

"Oh?" I dig my nails into my thigh as I wait for her to tell me more.

"I told you she has a memory like an elephant—that's what they say, right? She says your mother didn't die, at least not while she was at the facility."

"What?" I nearly choke on my tongue.

"Yeah, she was adamant about that. She doesn't know what happened, but she says there was no death. If there was, she would have processed the record—she remembers your mom specifically because she had one visitor who came every single week for visiting hours. A businessman who acted like he owned the place—she said he was so arrogant that all the nurses hated him."

"Oh," I say, my mind running away with the possibilities. "I . . . is she sure?"

"She's positive. She said she still has discharge papers and death records from that time. When the facility closed for good, they just left boxes of patient files in the records wing. She didn't want them to fall into bad hands, so she brought them all home. Most of them are still stored in her basement. She's going to have a look for you and then get back to me. I'll give you a call if she comes up with anything."

"Oh—okay" is all I can manage to say. "Thank you so much."

"Of course, hon. I'm sorry to be the bearer of bad news. I hope you find out what really happened."

"Yeah, thank you. You've been so helpful." I hang up, my mind filled with confusion.

If my mother didn't die at the facility, what did happen?

And why did my dad lie to me all these years?

"El! You home?" Jack interrupts my thoughts.

"In here," I reply from the kitchen.

"What are you up to?" He comes around the corner, pulls me into a half-hug, and then plants a kiss on the crown of my head. I have to suppress a cringe. His overly affectionate actions feel forced, especially since we've barely been speaking since our last fight. It's like he feels guilty about something.

"Researching the facility my mom was at," I reply.

"Oh." He pulls away, eyes glancing to my screen and then across the kitchen. "Why?"

"Dad never shared much about what happened, and I've always wondered. I mean, how does someone die in a facility that's meant to keep them safe from themselves and other people? Seems odd."

"Does it?" He takes a glass down from the cupboard and fills it with filtered water from the fridge.

"You don't think so?" I say, as he drinks the entire glass and then sets it in the sink.

He shrugs. "Not really. Maybe you're remembering wrong, El. It's the grief. It twists things." His eyes cut across the room to me. "Find anything interesting?"

"Not yet." I give him a sour smile. "Busy night?"

"Mm-hmm," he says, averting his eyes. "Drinks with a client went late."

He's lying. I clear my throat, then say, "They always do."

He arches one eyebrow but doesn't reply.

"Thought you were off to Jersey last night?" I smile sweetly at my lying husband as I stand, pushing in the barstool at the kitchen island and then tucking my laptop under my arm.

"Client cancelled," comes his dry reply.

"Hm. Well, I'm off to bed." I can't even look him in the eye.

"I'll be there soon." He grunts softly.

"Oh, you don't mind sleeping in the guest bedroom again, do you? I really liked having the bed to myself last night—I think I sleep better. It's nice to spread out. Plus, you snore." Jack doesn't snore. He's as still and as quiet as a corpse when he sleeps.

"Sure, if you think that's best."

"Thanks." I smile, letting a thousand words unspoken hang between us. "Good night."

"Sleep tight," I hear him murmur at my back.

Thanks, asshole, is all I think as I walk away.

TWENTY-FOUR

Ellie

"Here's your chamomile tea, dear." The barista sets a teacup and pot down at the table. "Let me know if I can get you anything else."

I smile up at her and nod. "Thanks."

I take my first sip of tea, enjoying the warmth in my system just as an older woman walks up with a manila folder and a smile. "Ellie?"

"Hi," I say. "You must be Rachel."

"I am; thank you for meeting me." She sits, pushing the folder across the table. "This is all my friend could find. I'm not sure if it's what you're looking for, but it's something."

"Thank you for meeting me—I appreciate it more than I can say." I smile, then open the folder and find a single sheet of paper. My mother's discharge paperwork. I scan the information, looking for any more details. No diagnosis, no list of medications, no forwarding address. Suddenly all hope I had vanishes like sand between my fingers.

"Do you know who she was discharged to?"

Rachel leans over the table, eyes on the signature line at the bottom of the file. "You don't recognize that signature?"

"No." I shake my head, trying to make out the slashes and swoops.

"Me either." She frowns. "I can't even make out the name."

"Probably on purpose," I grumble.

Rachel nods. "Look there."

She points to the last line of the document. I read it aloud. "Patient released into the custody of a private caregiver. All records destroyed." I meet Rachel's gaze. "Why would they destroy all of her records?"

"I wish I knew, hon." Rachel frowns. "She must have been released to someone important. Normally a doctor would need to sign off on a care sheet for the next facility or caregiver—it's an entire process."

"Do you think..." I trail off, thoughts running away with me.

"Do I think what?" She smiles.

"I don't know, I just . . . don't understand what happened. The story I was told was that she died in your facility."

Rachel shakes her head. "She was there for a while, but she didn't die there. I hate to say this but there was a lot of upheaval that year. The nursing strike, high turnover among doctors and nurses, and a revolving door of interns and patients . . . I'm not surprised there are records missing. I only worked there for nine months but every day was a mess, and I don't say that lightly."

Emotion starts to well in my eyes, but I shove it down. "I have so many questions."

"I know, me too." She pats my hand sympathetically. "I'm sorry this isn't what you were expecting. Maybe whoever told you that was mistaken."

"Maybe." Anxiety bubbles within me as awareness sinks in.

My mother didn't die in a psychiatric facility.

She vanished.

TWENTY-FIVE

Ellie

The cold wakes me.

At first, I don't know where I am. My bare legs are stiff with chill, and the thin cotton of my nightgown does nothing against the bite of early morning air.

I blink against the darkness, my breath fogging in front of me. Tile under me. Railings. The city sprawled below, a grid of blurred, blinking lights.

I'm outside. On the balcony.

My body jerks, heart slamming against my ribs. I scramble upright too fast, the wrought iron rail digging into the small of my back. My feet are freezing against the tile. My hair is damp with sweat—or maybe dew.

I clutch my arms around myself, spinning in a slow, horrified circle.

How did I get out here?

The last thing I remember is brushing my teeth, climbing into bed, turning off the lamp. Jack was still working late in his home office, the low hum of his voice carrying down the hall from his endless phone calls.

I didn't have wine. I wasn't dreaming.

And yet here I am.

The balcony table has been moved—pushed up against the railing like a step stool. The chair is angled strangely, pulled far back against the wall.

I stare at it, throat dry. I didn't move that table. I'm certain of it.

The sliding door behind me rattles open, making me jump. Jack stands there, backlit by the warm glow of the apartment, looking more annoyed than alarmed.

"Jesus, Ellie." He steps onto the balcony barefoot, wearing sweatpants and an old Columbia Law sweatshirt. "What the hell are you doing out here?"

I open my mouth but nothing comes out. He moves toward me, taking off his sweatshirt and draping it over my shoulders like I'm a child.

"You're freezing." He rubs my arms briskly, guiding me back toward the open door. "You had another episode, didn't you?"

"No—" My voice comes out hoarse, rough with cold and confusion. "I don't—I didn't—"

"Come on." His tone shifts, low and pitying. Like I'm fragile. Like I'm broken.

Like I'm the problem.

He steers me inside, closing the balcony door behind us. The warmth of the apartment feels suffocating.

"I told you this would happen," Jack says as he leads me to the couch. He crouches in front of me, smoothing hair back from my face with a careful hand. "You're under too much pressure. Work. All the sleepwalking and late nights. It's too much for you, El."

I stare past him, back at the balcony, at the table pushed to the railing, the chair shoved back awkwardly.

I didn't move them. I didn't climb up there. Someone moved them. Someone wanted them like that.

"Maybe you should call your therapist in the morning," Jack says gently. "Maybe you should go back on something. Just for a little while. Until you feel more like yourself again."

I nod, but my skin is crawling. Not from the cold anymore. From something worse.

Jack thinks he's winning. He thinks he's got me convinced that my mind is turning against me.

But he's wrong.

* * *

Later that afternoon Dr. Miriam Kessler sits across from me in a cream armchair, her legs crossed elegantly, a leather notebook balanced on one knee. She's beautiful in that polished, clinical way—tailored navy slacks, crisp white blouse, not a hair out of place. Even her smile feels rehearsed.

"The best in Manhattan," Jack had promised me, pressing the business card into my hand with the quiet urgency of someone offering a lifeline.

"You'll love her. She understands complicated things."

Complicated things.

Like psychotic breaks. Like neglect. Like being gaslit until you don't know which way is up.

I smooth my palms over my jeans and clear my throat. "I'm not sure where to start."

Dr. Kessler smiles encouragingly. "Start anywhere you like, Ellie. There's no wrong place to begin."

I stare at the pristine surface of her desk, at the gleaming crystal paperweight that pins down a stack of empty notecards. I pick a thread on my shirt carefully.

"I woke up outside on my balcony last night," I say. "I don't remember going out there. I was barefoot. Freezing."

Dr. Kessler nods, jotting something down. "Sleepwalking episodes can be common during periods of extreme stress."

I hesitate. "Yes. But . . ."

"But what?" Her pen is poised, ready.

"It's not just that," I say slowly. "Things move around in my apartment. Furniture. Objects. Little things. And I—" I falter, ashamed of the words even as they fall out of me. "I think someone might be doing it on purpose."

She tilts her head slightly, a movement so deliberate it feels staged. "You think someone's breaking into your apartment?"

"Maybe." My voice is barely above a whisper. "Or . . . maybe not breaking in. Maybe someone with access."

"Your husband?" she asks gently.

A warning prickles under my skin. The way she said it—not curious.

Leading.

I shift in my seat. "I don't know. I don't want to believe that."

"But you suspect it." She doesn't phrase it as a question.

I press my lips together. "I just . . . sometimes I feel like I'm being watched."

Dr. Kessler's gaze sharpens almost imperceptibly.

"Ellie, you've mentioned the core trauma of your mother's passing and how you've struggled with your father's silence surrounding that time." Her voice remains carefully neutral. "Sometimes trauma can create . . . false memories. Paranoia. Our minds try to shield us from painful truths by rewriting them."

False memories. *Paranoia.*

There it is.

The words hit me harder than a slap.

I stare at her, my mouth dry.

Jack said almost the same thing. After I started digging into the inconsistencies about my mother's death.

You're remembering wrong, El. It's the grief. It twists things.

I fidget with the hem of my sleeve, trying to keep my voice steady. "I remember seeing her being taken away. Men in white coats. She screamed at me not to believe my dad."

Dr. Kessler leans forward slightly, pen tapping once against her notebook. "Memories from childhood, especially traumatic ones, can be notoriously unreliable. It's possible you misinterpreted what you saw. Or that your father tried to shield you from the full truth for your own protection."

I feel myself slipping, the ground tilting under me.

Is she right? Am I losing it?

"I know what I saw," I say, but it sounds weak even to my own ears.

She offers a sympathetic smile. "Of course you believe you do. But, Ellie, let's consider: If your father truly wanted to hurt you—or your mother—why would he have cared for you all these years? Why would he have kept you safe, made sure you had the best education, the best life?"

Because it made him look good. Because it kept up appearances. Because control is easier when the prisoner thinks the warden loves them.

I bite down on the words.

"Have you considered," Dr. Kessler continues smoothly, "that your grief, combined with recent stressors, might be distorting your perception of those around you?"

A chill slips down my spine.

"Who recommended you to Jack?" I ask suddenly.

Her smile doesn't falter, but her eyes flicker—just for a second.

"We have mutual friends in the city. A lot of successful men and women come through my practice."

Mutual friends. Successful men. Like my father. Like Jack.

I stand up too quickly, the room tilting for a moment.

"Ellie," Dr. Kessler says carefully, "we're just starting to unpack a lot of deep-seated issues. I hope you'll trust the process. Sometimes healing can feel like betrayal to the wounded mind."

I nod like I'm agreeing. Like I'm grateful. But inside, something hardens. I don't trust her. I don't trust any of them. Jack didn't send me to be helped. He sent me to be silenced.

And whatever they're trying to bury—I'm going to dig it up.

TWENTY-SIX

Ellie

"Deeper. Cut deeper." Pain shoots through my arm. *"Deeper, don't stop."* More pain. More blood. Throbbing. Screaming. So much pain. *"Deeper!"*

My hand trembles as I hold a single shard of glass to my skin.

"Stop," I moan, tears burning my eyes. "Pleeeease."

My eyes shoot open, my vision hazy as the room comes into focus. The scent of blood fills my nostrils. I nearly choke on the coppery odor. I stumble, bumping into the counter and holding a hand out to catch myself. It's then that I see it. Rivers of red running down my arm and into the sink.

"Oh God," I groan, grabbing the nearest hand towel and wrapping it around my arm. I can't tell if the cuts are deep or superficial, but they're throbbing. I drop the bloody shard of wine glass into the sink and then unwrap my arm to have a quick look. Fuck. If I need stitches, it will be impossible to hide them from Jack. He'll never let me be again—he'll handcuff me to him and drive me straight to the asylum.

I hold my wrapped arm to me and move to the bathroom. I find bandages in the drawer, and antibiotic ointment. I move quickly, trying my best to keep the dripping blood limited to the sink as I squirt the ointment over my arm and then begin wrapping the wound tightly. It takes me a few minutes, but finally the bandages are tight enough that the blood isn't seeping through. I glance down at the bloody towel in the sink, thinking that it looks like a crime scene in here. I'll have to wash everything up and clean the sink and discard the wine glass before Jack gets home.

And then it occurs to me what's going on here. It's the middle of the night. I was sleepwalking and just about ended my own life with a broken wine glass. Maybe Jack is right: Maybe I can't be trusted when left alone. Maybe if I knew what was good for me, I would take myself to the psychiatric facility. Bare minimum I could use some new medications to help me sleep peacefully.

I cringe as I gather the bloody towel and take it to the washing machine. I toss it in, add soap, and hit start before heading to the kitchen to clean up the broken glass. My eyes ache with exhaustion by the time I'm finished. It's after four a.m. by the time I go back to bed, my arm throbbing.

When I wake a few hours later, my head is foggy and the only thing I know for sure is that work would be all but impossible today. From bed, I shoot a quick email off to Human Resources and explain that I'm feeling under the weather. Then I open an internet search bar and begin researching severe sleepwalking disorders.

I'm deep down the rabbit hole reading an article about a woman who used a sleep disorder defense in a murder case when I hear the front door open. My heart lurches because no one should be coming into the house in the middle of the morning on a Friday. I move to the bedroom door and peek through the crack, my heart calming when I see my husband walking through the kitchen. I pull the sleeve of my sweatshirt down to cover my bandages and then open the door.

"Hey!" I call as I walk into the kitchen.

Jack jumps, spinning around with a look of shock on his features. "What are you doing here?"

"I didn't feel good this morning—I had trouble sleeping last night," I confess. He looks me up and down, as if he's trying to find the lie in my words. "You okay?"

"Yeah." I tug at my sleeve subconsciously, sending him a reassuring but fake smile.

"Hey—don't forget about that juicing retreat I bought you for your birthday." He sets his laptop bag down on the counter.

"Oh, right. When is it again?"

"This weekend." He pulls something out of his pocket, opening the trash can to dispose of it. "What's this?"

"Hm?" I settle at the kitchen island, my mind hazy with the lack of sleep.

"A broken wine glass . . . covered in blood?" His eyes narrow on mine.

"Oh—yeah, happened last night." I try to make light of the situation.

"Is that so?" Jack closes the trash can and then moves closer to me, eyes lingering on the sleeve of my sweatshirt. "Did you cut yourself?"

I glance down at my sleeve to find fresh blood staining the hem.

"Yeah—it's nothing." I force a smile.

"Doesn't look like nothing," he grunts, grasping my arm and pulling it toward him. I wince at the pain, thinking not for the first time that maybe I should have gone to the emergency room to get stitches last night. "Jesus, El—" He shoves my sleeve up to reveal my poorly bandaged and bloody arm. "What the fuck?"

"I'm fine." I yank my arm out of his grip and pull my sleeve down. "I just need to switch out the bandage."

Jack's eyes pierce mine with a dozen unsaid accusations. He finally seems to land on one and says, "It's like you're fucking possessed at night."

"Really?" I spit with anger.

"Really, El. I think digging into your past is dredging up old harmful memories. I mean, what else am I supposed to think? I asked you to take some time off from work and maybe do a spa getaway, see a doctor about some sleep medications—"

"Sleep medications can make sleepwalking worse, actually—I've been reading."

"Right." He huffs, slamming his open palm down on the counter. "I'm doing what I can to keep you safe, but it's like you don't even care for your own safety—why the hell should I?" He pushes a hand through his hair. "You remember that time you were put on a seven-day hold in high school? You tried to take your own life, El."

"That's not true—" I protest, but the words fall flat when I realize I don't really remember why I was there. Oh, I remember the facility, all right—the facility, the meds, the nurses, the endless tests—but I don't remember *why* I was committed. There's a giant black hole in my memory.

"Oh my God—" I say, about to level him with an accusation, before I realize it's just better if I keep my mouth shut. And then another possibility occurs to me.

Aubrey—is she more than just a friendly neighbor who might be having an affair with my husband? Maybe Jack put her up to babysitting me.

I can't shake the thought as I consider all the things she's said to me, plus the fact that they were both at the Peninsula that night. Maybe they were meeting for a check-in somewhere safe, somewhere they didn't think I'd find them.

"You know, I've done my share of research too. Even called one of the psychiatrists in the city who your father recommended—he says sleepwalking is genetic. Madness runs in families, El. There's nothing to be ashamed of—we just need to do what we can to treat you, give you some peace... hell, give *me* some peace."

Is he right? Is history repeating itself? I feel like I've been under a microscope these last few months, paranoia about my illness reaching a fever pitch as I try to dodge the landmines of my genetics.

But I can't shake the feeling that something is off—like Jack is lying to me. Or that he at least has an ulterior motive of wanting to rid himself of me, maybe so he and Aubrey can run off into the sunset together.

Is this how it ends? The undoing of my marriage? A slow descent into chaos and pain before one last blow takes us out for good? Or maybe it was already undone, the emotional affair dismantling what was left of us.

TWENTY-SEVEN

Ellie

"Fresh carrot juice aligns the chakras and balances the heart center." The woman doing the juicing demonstration is swirling the vibrant juice in the glass with a smile.

I have to suppress a groan. This hippie lifestyle is not for me; I'm not sure what Jack was thinking—only that he was desperate to get me out of the house for the weekend, I guess. I'm sure he's at the end of his rope, and since I've been refusing any further treatment for the sleepwalking, this seems like a last-ditch effort to get me help. To be honest, though, I think I'd rather be at an inpatient facility for a week than try to smile my way through all this juicing for your chakras bullshit.

The woman drones on, and I start to shift in my seat, glancing at the group of a half dozen or so other women around me. Is anyone else as tortured as I am? It's been exactly three hours since I left the city, and already it's taking everything in me to not call an Uber to get home. I sip the small shot glass of beet juice that was passed out as soon as our group sat down, my eyes traveling out to the line of evergreens in the distance. I'm only thirty minutes or so from Kat's Westchester estate, Tempsford Manor.

I have half a mind to Uber over there and ask Kat directly about the delivery of milk and honey that was sent to my doorstep a few days ago, but then, Kat probably isn't even there. As far as I can tell, she spends all week long in the city doing charity events and lunches at chic eateries like Le Bernardin. On second thought, though, maybe checking out Kat's estate on my own is exactly what I should do. I could feign ignorance to the staff if anyone caught me wandering around, investigating ... what?

My thoughts are interrupted by a preppy thirty-something with a smile asking me if I want to be her partner for goat yoga.

"I—I'm actually not feeling great. I think I have to pass; thank you, though." The woman wrinkles her nose at me as if I'm speaking another language. I guess women like her aren't used to being turned down. I add in my most enthusiastic voice: "It sounds so fun, though! I hope you love it!"

That seems to cheer her up because her smile brightens. "Hope you feel better soon!"

I nod, wave, and then stand from the chair, thinking the sooner I get myself back to the city, the better. I move in the opposite direction of the rest of the group, sipping their fresh beet and carrot juice as they saunter over to the goat yoga segment of the weekend. As I make my way up to my bedroom in the boutique B and B, I order a car to take me back to the city. I grab my overnight bag before heading back downstairs and right out the front doors.

I feel a little bad that Jack's birthday gift will go to waste, but these are not my people. In fact, maybe I'll book a weekend at my favorite spa in the city—a massage, facial, and some sushi sounds way more relaxing. All of this fresh-pressed juice is turning my stomach—and I'm supposed to do this all weekend? Without real food? It's taken me two hours to come to the conclusion that juicing is bullshit. If it wasn't for the weird place Jack and I have been in lately I probably would have said that exactly, but I didn't want to seem ungrateful for his gift. But then . . . if he knew me at all, he would've known this isn't my bag.

The drive from Peekskill back to the city takes just over an hour, long enough for me to curse Jack for sending me way upstate. I tried to schedule a massage and facial at that day spa I like in the city, but they're booked through the rest of the month. I'd probably be too stressed to relax anyway, my mind churning over all that's been going on lately. I think of the milk tucked away in the fridge. What if Jack got ahold of it by mistake? Maybe then all of my problems would be solved—or maybe they'd just be beginning.

By the time I climb the stairs to our second-floor apartment, I've decided to send Kat a quick email and demand to know more about the grocery delivery that landed on my doorstep a few days ago. All of that changes, however, when I walk into the apartment and find Jack's work files spread out on the kitchen table. I cross the room, eyes trained on the array of folders. At least half a dozen different stacks are perched precariously on the table; more folders are spread wide open in various arrangements. I catch sight of my father's name on one of the top files and I can't help but open the folder, my curiosity piqued. I flip through the first few pages of paperwork, and then I shiver.

Check stubs peer back at me. Settlements made out to different women. Receipts for endowments to Columbia University and, lastly, a paystub made out to my husband from Cayman National Bank. Of course my father has an offshore bank account in the Cayman Islands he hasn't told me about—it's probably not the only one—but could my husband also have one?

A sudden feeling of being naïve washes over me. I flip through a few more papers and find more stubs of checks made out to my husband—for staggering amounts. Most are more than his yearly salary.

And the worst part? Some are dated before Jack and I even met.

TWENTY-EIGHT

Ellie

I haven't seen Jack in two days. Not since I found all of the financial files that don't make sense. I don't know where he's been staying—it certainly hasn't been at the apartment. I imagine he's staying at his office. I spent all day Sunday hibernating in bed and ruminating on all the things I don't know about my husband. I even searched the local real estate market for two-bedrooms with a view of the park, briefly entertaining the idea of selling everything and starting over somewhere else. I've never asked much about my father and Jack's business dealings, but now I'm thinking I should have. It's hard to fathom leaving Jack and living alone—I've never lived by myself—but then, what choice do I have? I can't just sit here with my head in the sand, can I?

I considered talking to my dad about it—he's the only other person I trust—but I don't even trust him anymore. The truth is I don't know who to trust. My faith has been rocked—I feel like every instinct I have about people has been wrong. I think about all the questions I have for my father, and about the fact that The Society expects my next target to be him. I haven't parsed out all of the details, but I know one thing for sure: I can't rely on anyone but myself in this life.

"El—delivery!" one of the executive assistants calls through the crack in my door.

My heart sinks. I'm like Pavlov's dog when it comes to deliveries now—my anxiety skyrockets each time a box lands on my doorstep, whether it's at home or the office.

I haul myself out of my desk chair and walk the short distance to the assistant's desk to find a large box waiting for me.

"Looks like someone was up all night ordering some goodies." Her eyes dart to the box and then to me.

I ignore her and lift the box. It's heavy. I curse under my breath as I walk with it back to my office. I close the door because I know I'm going to need privacy for whatever this is. I cut the tape on the box with a letter opener and then groan when I find more glass bottles of milk, cream, and honey. On top of everything sits a note that says:

If you don't do it, you'll regret it.

I swallow, hands trembling as I hold the note in my hands. It's obviously from The Society. They clearly don't like that I haven't answered their emails and haven't made a move on my father. Maybe I should send a quick email and explain that I have a conflict of interest with this target. I think about how to explain that I can't take down the next rapist asshole on their list because he raised me. Tucked me in at night, showed up at my dance recitals, shared every holiday dinner with me and still does . . .

This is without a doubt the reason I was chosen. My heart hurts at the thought. If he's guilty, how can I let him get away with hurting people? And if he's not . . . how am I supposed to escape the overbearing clutches of these powerful women in The Society? I'm not even sure how to find out the truth of the situation. I can't exactly ask. I think then of Aubrey and the police reports from the women accusing my father of horrendous abuses. Is it true? Could the documents have been altered?

I shove the note back into the box and close it, walking it straight out of my door and to the trash chute across the office. I don't care who knows, who finds out, who gets angry; threat or no threat, I have no intention of giving my father this gift—no matter how harmless it may seem.

By the time I'm back at my desk my mind is whirring with all the possibilities I may not have considered. As soon as I sit down, I open a new internet search window and type in the name "Aubrey Collins." It takes me exactly ten minutes to come to the conclusion that there is no evidence of her on the internet—no social media profiles, no LinkedIn with a work history—nothing. She's practically a ghost as far as the internet is concerned—and it's basically impossible not to have left a trail on the internet these days.

My heart sinks as I think back on all the things I've told her, all the time we've spent together. Who is she? Why is she here? It occurs to me then that I wouldn't put it past my father to hire someone to watch out for me. He's been worried for a long time about my mental stability—would he go so far as to hire a caregiver like Aubrey on the quiet to keep an eye on me?

By the time lunch comes, I haven't focused for more than a minute at a time, so I send an email to my manager saying I'll be working from home the rest of the day. Maybe even the rest of the week. Maybe forever.

TWENTY-NINE

Ellie

I wake with a jolt. My heart hammers and my throat is dry. I search my memory for a dream or a nightmare that woke me, but I can't remember anything. My arm is throbbing and the bandage feels damp, like it needs to be changed. I think again that maybe I should have gone to the hospital for stitches, but I can't face the fact that I might be hurting myself at night, on top of everything else.

Correction: I *am* hurting myself.

I push out of bed, finding the sheets damp with sweat. Whatever I was dreaming about must have been stressful. It's not even two in the morning and I feel like I've been asleep for days. I rub the sleep from my eyes and make my way to the bathroom. I splash my face with cold water and then make quick work of changing the bandage on my arm. My stomach growls, reminding me that I didn't have anything to eat all day. I pad to the kitchen, the realization hitting me that despite the fact that Jack hasn't been home much at all these last few months, it's still weird to wake up in the middle of the night and not have him here.

This is what being single feels like, I think. No one else to remind you to eat dinner or to drive you to the emergency room when you have a sleepwalking episode that turns bloody. I grab a bottle of Advil from the cupboard and swallow two of them with orange juice, then hunt through the fridge for anything to eat. I decide on a sandwich and pull mustard, sliced turkey, and cheese from the drawer and a loaf of sourdough from the bin. I move to the kitchen island and pull a butter knife from the drawer, turning back to my bread on the counter before my eyes land on something unusual.

I gasp, the knife falling from my hand and clattering into the sink.

It's a gun. A shiny, gunmetal-colored handgun lying in my sink as if it belongs there. Or as if someone had been cleaning it and then just stepped away for a moment.

"What the fuck?" I whisper, leaning closer to inspect the weapon. *Maybe it's fake*, I think. But nothing about this gun looks fake. My fingers tremble as I reach out to touch it, but then think better at the last minute. I'll need to call the police. I've never been around guns, and to my knowledge neither has Jack. What if I'm wrong, though? What if this is just another secret he's been keeping from me?

My legs go weak and I plant a hand on the counter to keep myself from falling. My arm is suddenly throbbing again, right along with my brain. What is going on? Did *I* do this?

And then I think of the threatening note that came with the box of cream and honey earlier.

If you don't do it, you'll regret it.

Is this what they meant? And then a more terrifying realization hits me: Either I did this while I was sleepwalking . . . or someone was *in* my apartment while I slept.

Fear throttles my system.

Did Jack do this? Aubrey? Or could it be the person who's been stalking me? Or maybe it was a member of The Society—just how much pull do those well-heeled women have?

I leave the gun where it is, return the sandwich stuff to the fridge, and then go to my laptop and open the news tab. It takes me exactly two minutes to come across a headline that's less than an hour old. *The New York Post* is reporting that the CEO of a Fortune 500 company was gunned down outside of his townhome on the Upper West Side just hours ago. I recognize the building, now cordoned off with police tape. Investigators are lingering around the front doors. A quick skim of the article tells me that no perpetrator has been identified and the only thing they know about the crime is that the CEO was shot at close range with a handgun. A handgun that hasn't been found.

I close my laptop, not bothering to read more as a chill of awareness works its way through me.

I don't need to read anything else because I have a feeling I know where the missing handgun is: in my sink. I just don't know who it belongs to, or who put it there.

The only thing I know for sure is that someone is trying to frame me for the kind of crime that will dominate the headlines for weeks.

I suddenly wish my husband was here for a hug, to tell me that everything is going to be okay. That I didn't do this and that there is some reasonable explanation for a handgun to find its way into my sink in the middle of the night. But even if he did tell me what I want to hear, it would all be lies. Because there is no reasonable explanation. My door locks automatically with a keycode required for access. It's unlikely someone let themselves into my apartment just to plant a weapon and leave. No, the most obvious explanation is that I was sleepwalking and found the gun somewhere. I remember waking up to the sweat-soaked sheets, my heart pounding as if cortisol had been shuttling through my system for hours—almost as if I'd been out running a midnight marathon.

I go to the bathroom, taking in my reflection in the mirror. I look disheveled, strung out—like a junkie who hasn't slept in days. I flip on the cold water and splash my face again, hoping to wash away the stress, hoping that the next time I look in the mirror, the girl I used to know will be standing there looking back at me. The one with an easy, boring life.

But when I look up, there's only me. With blood on my hands.

THIRTY

Ellie

I can't stop thinking about the gun in my sink.

Every time I close my eyes I see the shiny gunmetal as if it's tattooed on the back of my eyelids. My knees feel weak and my hands won't stop shaking. The knowledge that I could have done something criminal is too much. Was I sleepwalking again? Did I have a blackout?

Maybe . . . maybe I really did kill the CEO.

The thought crashes through my chest, hot and wild.

The news said he was shot execution-style as he was stepping out of the lobby—like a professional hit. No security footage. No suspect. And now a gun—this gun—is in my sink, like a calling card I don't remember writing.

Am I breaking?

Just like my mother?

I think of Jack's accusations that I'm unraveling. Maybe he's right. Maybe I can't tell what's real and what's imagined.

You need professional help, El. His tone cold and detached, like he was already mourning who I used to be.

But now I know better. Jack isn't mourning. Jack is lying.

Every nerve in my body blares like a siren at the memory of all that money in the Grand Cayman accounts. And now there's a gun in my sink.

I clutch the countertop until my knuckles ache. The kitchen is dark except for the streetlight bleeding through the blinds, casting illuminated stripes across the cabinets. Everything in me is begging for logic, but there's nothing logical about this. I can't help but wonder what other secrets are hiding right under my nose. I begin searching the apartment.

Every drawer. Every crevice. I start with the usual places—front closet, shoeboxes, bedside tables—but it's Jack's things I'm drawn to. His home office. His leather laptop bag. The filing cabinet he never gave me the passcode to. For hours, I tear through his life, page by page.

Tax returns. Contracts. Dry-cleaning slips. All normal. All expected. Except it's not.

I know there's more. I just have to find it.

Around 5:30 a.m., just as dawn spills across the sky, I find it—hidden behind his Columbia diploma on the bottom shelf of the bookcase. A small black safe, bolted into the wall. I almost miss it, until the light catches the edge of the keypad.

I stare at it, pulse hammering. My mind starts running through possible codes he might have used.

His birthday. Our anniversary. The date he started his first job. It clicks open on the third try: the day of our first date. Inside is a passport and a sleek, unfamiliar laptop.

The passport photo is him—but not his name.

Julian McCallister. Canadian. Born in Montreal. Forty-two years old.

It takes a full minute before I can breathe again.

Julian McCallister. I flip through the passport, fingers trembling. Multiple stamps from the Cayman Islands. Germany. Singapore.

I remember the offshore accounts I found. So much money funneled from my father to him. God help me, I believed everything.

I open the laptop. Password protected. But Jack—or Julian—is so predictable. His favorite author's name, all lowercase, gets me in.

What I find makes my heart stop.

Thousands of files. Financial spreadsheets, encrypted communications, hidden work documents I've never seen before. And security footage. Dozens of folders, each labeled with a date. My hand hovers over the most recent.

Today.

I click.

The screen splits into four feeds. Living room. Kitchen. Bedroom. Bathroom.

My knees nearly buckle. It's me. It's me standing at the kitchen sink. Just seconds ago. Recorded. Archived. Watched.

He's been spying on me.

Not just for days. Or weeks.

For a year.

A year ago—when I had the emotional affair. When I thought Jack had grown distant and cold and I turned to someone else for comfort. We never touched, but we talked. About everything. About Jack.

Jack heard it all.

He saw it all.

Every conversation. Every private moment. Every breakdown. Every night I curled into myself and cried in the shower.

All of it.

And Aubrey. She's in the footage too. In our apartment. Laughing with me on the couch. Telling me I'm too good for Jack. Hugging me. Sharing wine as we bitched about men and life and love.

I step back from the desk, dizzy. The air feels thick, poisoned.

I think of my father. Of how he told me my mother died in that psychiatric facility when I was seven. But she didn't.

He lied. Just like Jack. Why?

And what else are they hiding from me?

The psychiatric facility closed years ago—its records scattered, shredded, buried. But maybe my father knows more than he admits. Maybe he and Jack have always known more than they say.

My father vouched for Jack when we met. Said he was trustworthy. Loyal.

"Just like me," he'd said about his new intern.

Maybe that's the problem.

They're exactly alike.

A chill slithers down my spine. I think of my father's penthouse, high above the city, his fortress of privilege and control. What does he keep there? Files? Photos? Anything about my mother? Maybe it's time I find out.

I tuck the fake passport into my sweatshirt pocket. My reflection glimmers in the dark laptop screen, fractured and unfamiliar. I'm not sure who I am anymore. A grieving daughter? A cheating wife? A murderer?

The gun is still in the sink. I glance toward the kitchen and wonder again if it's the same one used to kill that CEO. If I touch it again, am I leaving my fingerprints, or were they already there?

I don't know what's real. But I know what I have to do next. Jack—Julian—thinks he's been watching me. But now I'm watching him.

THIRTY-ONE

Ellie

My phone vibrates to life on Jack's desk. I cross the room and swipe at the screen. Another anonymous message.

Don't make me angry. You won't like me when I'm angry.

My heart stops for a few long beats. I hit delete on the message. Maybe I should change my phone number. Maybe it's time to uproot my entire life and start over—new job, new city, new me. Heck, maybe I even need a new name to escape the legacy I was born into. I'm not sure what's fiction and what's reality anymore—am I going crazy or is it everyone around me that can't be trusted? Maybe it's both.

I think of the possible suspects who could be sending me these threatening messages. The list is long—too long. My instinct is to lock myself in this apartment forever, not that that would do much good.

I snap a quick picture of Jack's fake passport—or is it his real one and the man I'm married to isn't Jack at all? I email a few of the security files to my own computer for later. I'm not sure I'll ever have a use for them, but I need to know they're real—that this isn't just something else my broken mind is manufacturing. I shove Jack's secret laptop back where I found it and stumble out to the kitchen, headed straight for the sink just to confirm that the gun is real and right where I left it.

It glints back at me in the early morning light. I don't know what to do. My instinct is to reach out to The Society and tell them what I've found, but then, I don't even think I can trust them. Women like that don't take well to being ignored, and I still haven't figured out what I'm supposed to do about my dad. Is he really the villain when he's the only person who's been here, supporting me for all of my life? Where would I be without him? I can't even begin to fathom.

No—revealing anything to The Society isn't the right move. They already know far more about me than I'm comfortable with, and what do I know about them? Practically nothing. Kat speaks like they're a loving, supportive family, but the more I know these women the more secrets they seem to keep. It's not lost on me that I'm expected to trust them, but they don't seem to trust me with anything other than doing their dirty work. I'm only a pawn in their revenge games.

My breathing grows ragged and shallow as thoughts swirl uncontrollably in my mind. Who can I trust? Who has it out for me? Who's threatening me with anonymous text messages? I head back to my bedroom and straight for the walk-in closet. I pull a backpack off the shelf and shove a few changes of clothes into it along with my phone charger and laptop, then pull a pair of denim shorts on before going straight for the front door. My heart is hammering a chaotic rhythm behind my ribs and I can't seem to catch a breath as I open the door and run straight into Aubrey.

"Oh—El—hi. I was just coming to check on you." Warmth pools in her green eyes.

My phone vibrates with another notification then.

If I can't have you, no one can . . .

I shove the phone deep in my bag as fear and panic overtake me. "I—I—" I press my lips together, sucking in a breath through my nose. My eyes flutter closed as my muscles tense with anxiety. I claw at my shirt, desperate for air. "I can't breathe."

"What? El—God—" She pulls the backpack from my shoulder and then guides me down to sit on the floor. "Deep breaths—just take nice, slow, deep breaths."

I nod, trying to suck in lungfuls of air through my nose. "I—I need to get away from this apartment."

"Oh, honey—" Aubrey pulls me into a hug, rubbing my back in slow circles just like a mother comforting a child. I let her. "Why don't you come to my place and tell me what's wrong?"

I nod, because I don't know what else to do. I have nowhere to go, no one to trust. She plants a hand on my arm and gently raises me to my feet. With my backpack hung over her shoulder and our fingers laced together, she walks me down the hallway to her apartment.

Once we're inside, she guides me to the sleek leather couch that overlooks West 60th and brings me a cold bottle of water. "I'll let Jack know you're safe with me—"

"No!" I bark, shaking my head desperately. "Please, don't. I just . . . I just found out some things and I don't know what to think or what to do . . . I just . . . I don't think I know my husband like I thought I did."

Aubrey frowns, eyebrows scrunched together as she takes

me in. I see her visibly swallow before she plops down on the couch next to me. She rubs my knee softly, and then sighs.

"I was waiting for this..."

"What?" I blink away more tears as my mind spins with a thousand thoughts.

"El, Jack isn't who he says he is."

My heart thunders like a freight train in my ears, my vision tunneling to her sympathetic gaze holding mine. "Is anyone?"

A wry chuckle escapes her lips. "Well..." She presses her lips together as if she's trying to keep the words from slipping out and ruining my life. "You got me there." Silence hangs a few long beats before her expression darkens. "El—I'm..." She squeezes my hand, then sighs. "I'm not who you think either."

"Oh God..." Anxiety causes butterflies to riot in my stomach. "Who then?"

She sniffs. Looks out the window at the morning traffic turning off Broadway onto 60th. "This isn't the right time, but God, I guess there's never a right time for a confession like this..."

"Please, just out with it already," I plead.

She nods, eyes swinging back to meet mine. "I'm your sister."

THIRTY-TWO

Aubrey

Pain fills Ellie's face as I make my confession. It's like I've landed a death blow and the air is vacating her lungs. I knew this moment would come. I didn't know when, I didn't know how. It's all for the best, though—this woman had to find out one way or another that she's been living a lie. So be it if I'm the catalyst. I don't mind being the villain in Ellie's life—not if it gets me a little closer to my goal. Oh, the twisted web I've managed to weave. Just wait until she finds out the rest of her pathetic reality.

"H-how?" she finally sputters.

I feel bad for her—I do—but not enough to continue the charade. "My mom was interning for the summer when she met your dad. He offered to drive her home one night when her car wouldn't start. He raped her in the back seat. I came screaming into this world nine months later." I tip my chin up, just daring her to challenge my version of events. "She was only twenty-three and he was forty-four. She tried to press charges but your father's lawyers buried her in accusations and smear campaigns. She ended up rescinding her allegations, but that did no good because she still got fired. He ruined her."

"How old are you?" Ellie finally thinks to ask.

"I just turned twenty-seven," I tell her.

She presses her lips together, shaking her head with disbelief. "I don't believe you."

I raise my eyebrows. Of course she doesn't. Ellie is stubborn and spoiled, used to living her life in a safe little bubble—but I've come to pop it. "I grew up across the river in North Bergen. My first fifteen years we lived in low-income housing and I went to a private school on grants. And then my mom married my stepdad, and he abused me until I was seventeen. I ran away and haven't looked back since."

"Prove it." El's tone is arrogant.

"I don't really know how you expect me to do that . . ." I think of my birth certificate, the line for father left blank—the glaring missing piece in my lineage. "My mom didn't tell me who my real father was until I was a teenager; from that point forward I became obsessed. With him. With you. With your lives here. With everything that was withheld from me. I used to put myself in your shoes, dream of what it would be like to live in a penthouse with a nanny and dance classes and a degree from Columbia."

Ellie tilts her head, her eyes narrowing with anger.

"I've been watching, waiting, dreaming of telling you the truth. Wondering if we'd get along, what it would be like to have a sister. And then I realized I'm your sister from the other side of the tracks. I grew up in your shadow, and for years I was fixated on why your father chose you and why he didn't choose me. Why he didn't love me like he did you."

"Maybe he didn't know about you. Maybe your mom was lying," Ellie snaps.

I shake my head, rage bubbling to life in my system. "Or maybe he's just a piece of shit."

Ellie glares at me, a mix of anger, resentment, and pain swirling in her hazel irises. She's so like me, but not. It's like staring into a mirror with a slightly distorted reflection. Her lips press into a thin line before she finally says, "I don't believe you."

I suck in a breath, squaring my shoulders and turning to face her fully. "That's understandable," I say. "I think it's better if I show you, then."

THIRTY-THREE

Ellie

The cab pulls up to a nondescript townhome in the West Village an hour after Aubrey's big reveal. *My sister.* My mind is numb, my body moving on autopilot. I wish, not for the first time, that I had someone else—*anyone else*—to turn to right now. I insulated myself, built a nest and made Jack and my father my everything. I didn't think I needed anyone else. But I couldn't have been more wrong.

"Thanks." Aubrey passes the cab driver a few bills, and we both step out onto the curb silently.

I cross my arms over my chest like a shield, as if that could protect me from any more emotional blows directed at me today. I don't think I have the heart for any more truths, but I'm not sure I can withstand any more lies either.

I follow Aubrey to the front stoop and watch as she punches a button on a small intercom. It crackles to life when a soft, Spanish-inflected voice greets us. Aubrey talks into the speaker, stating that we're here on "Society business," and the door buzzes, then clicks as it unlocks. She pushes the door open and we step into the most beautiful foyer I've ever seen.

The mansion is expansive—much bigger and more opulent than it looks from the outside. Dark navy embossed wallpaper stretches as far as the eye can see; rich cherry crown molding and an elegant chair rail offset the decor. Black and white art deco tiles stretch down the hallway, and chic gold frames and furnishings lend the space an old-Hollywood aesthetic that feels lavish and inviting at the same time.

"This is stunning," I say, eyes casting around the elegant space.

"Why thank you, dear." Words lodge in my throat when Kat appears as if out of nowhere. "Welcome to my home."

I nod, eyes wide with shock as she pulls me into a hug. "I'm so glad you like what you see. It will all be yours someday, after all."

"Excuse me?"

She holds me at arm's length, her warm gaze softening with sympathy as she directs her next words at Aubrey. "I see you haven't told her much."

My eyes bounce back and forth between the two women.

Kat continues, turning her attention to me. "I suppose I should formally introduce myself—*or reintroduce myself*, as it were." A saccharine smile lifts her cheeks. "I was born Ekaterina Volkov," she says, pausing a beat. When she doesn't seem to get the reaction she's looking for out of me, she continues. "But you might know me better as Valeria Thomas."

My heart stutters. Valeria Thomas is my mother's name. I must have misheard. "No." I shake my head as shock, doubt, and confusion spin in a perfect storm in my mind. "No way."

"First—would you like some tea? I always feel that tea or champagne helps a tough conversation go down a little more smoothly."

I nod, my gaze slicing across the room to linger on the glossy tile floors. Every cell in my body is vibrating with anxious energy. The urge to turn and run for the door is strong, but my desire to hear what else she might say outweighs everything else. "Champagne, please."

Kat calls for her housemaid. A short woman of Latin descent appears from a room down the hall. "Yes, ma'am?"

"Magda—could you bring a bottle of Moët and three flutes to the sitting room?"

The shorter woman nods, vanishing back into what I assume is the kitchen.

"Come." Kat waves for Aubrey and me to follow her. We move silently into the sitting room, where the polished parquet floors and rich velvet settees offset a fireplace that is nearly as tall as I am. She gestures for us to settle across from her on one of the sofas. She crosses her legs, folds her hands together, and rests them on her knee before Magda returns with a serving tray of champagne and flutes, pouring us each a glass. "Thank you, Magda."

Kat lifts her glass in a gesture of cheers. "To newfound friends and family."

I'm hardly able to hold back tears as I swallow the bubbly liquid.

"You must have so many questions," she begins.

I nod, at a loss for where to even start.

"First, I want you to know that I would never lie to you." Kat's smile feels less than authentic, as if she's trying to manufacture a genuine sentiment. I don't believe her. In fact, I don't really have faith that this woman has a genuine or authentic bone in her body. "What I'm about to tell you will be shocking; truth is so much stranger than fiction, don't you think?" Kat sips again and then sets her glass down.

I don't reply. I don't want to give this woman any more of me than I have to.

"I want to start by saying I know what you've been told." She holds my gaze for a few long beats. "And none of it is true." She pauses, waiting for my reaction. When I don't give her one, she continues, "Your father staged my mental breakdown to discredit me. He paid a psychiatrist a large sum of money to have me declared unfit—a harm to myself and you. As if I would ever hurt my own child."

"Why would he do that?" I don't bother to hide the disdain in my tone.

"Why wouldn't he?" Anger bleeds through her words. She sighs, then makes an effort to explain further. "For starters, if he can discredit me, he doesn't have to pay me a red cent for a divorce. If I simply just . . . vanish, he's off the hook for his responsibilities."

"That sounds like bullshit. The man you're describing isn't the man I know, the man who raised me."

"I understand that it looks that way from your perspective, but the version of events you've been fed has been carefully curated, Elyse."

"Why would I believe you? I don't even know you," I say.

"You have to understand—making a problem disappear for a man like him is much easier than following the regular course of events that most people are used to. Having his reputation destroyed with accusations of abuse and infidelity would be far worse for his business and public persona than having a wife who had a psychotic break. The first would encourage mistrust of his decision-making and ability to lead a multimillion-dollar business—can you imagine if the gossip columns knew the truth? He'd struggle to convince investors to give him all the money required to keep his businesses afloat. A crazy wife, on the other hand, elicits sympathy. Add into the mix a young daughter he's raising on his own and you have a recipe for continued success. People want to invest in a man they like. Your father is a smart man—the smartest I've ever met. It's one of the things I loved most about him in the beginning, and it's the very thing that destroyed me in the end."

I don't say anything. I just sit there in shock. The knowledge that I am related to both of these women is unnerving. Even more so because they knew. They played me. They withheld the truth and manipulated me like a puppet on a string. Resentment surges in me. I can't help it—I feel betrayed. And I feel like it's my time to do something about it, but what, I'm not sure. My hands feel tied—but only because I've tied them with my own naivete and willingness to place trust in people I never really knew.

"What are you thinking?" Kat interrupts my thoughts.

I swallow my resentment, as I try to put into words what I'm feeling. "I don't know what to say, to be honest."

"That's to be expected, I suppose." Kat's expression is sober.

Aubrey clears her throat, gaze hanging on Kat's before she turns to me, a look of empathy on her face as she takes in my silence. "I think you should know something else . . ." she begins. "Your mother—Kat"—she gestures to the woman across from us—"she founded The Society. She's the driving force behind our mission. In the years I've known her"—my eyes widen with Aubrey's admission that she's known my mother far longer than she previously let on—"she's always been an advocate for women, but after our father managed to have her committed to a psychiatric facility—after he tried to obliterate her and remove her from society, take her life from her to protect his own selfish interests—she made it official. Remember I told you that my mom was an intern when your father raped her?"

I nod.

"She was an intern at Greystone Psychiatric. After Daniel Thomas raped her, she helped your mother escape. That's why my mom lost her job—helping your mom. She knew your mom wasn't crazy—my mom had been raped by your mom's husband, so she knew he was a predator capable of anything." Aubrey's features are tight, controlled. "When your mom left Greystone Psychiatric, she started The Society. She took back her power and went from a fragile victim to a sharp, calculating woman."

I glance from Aubrey to the woman who claims to be my mother. I have no words for all I've been told in the last hour. My world has shifted on its axis. My life has always been simple and straightforward, but now I wonder if I was merely a victim of a fantasy that was told to me. My sense of safety was fabricated. My perspective begins to shift as I realize my mother—if she is who she claims to be—turned her victimhood into something shrewd and dangerous. She became a woman capable of ending the lives of men.

"How do I know what you're saying is real and not just more lies?" I finally ask her.

"Do you know anything about your past? Names, histories, and the like?"

"I know some things," I say.

"Did your father tell you that I was born in a small village in Slovenia? That we met when I was on a visa here in New York working for a modeling agency when I was nineteen? That your grandmother's name was Valentinja, and that I was born in the same small cottage she was born in—the same one my grandmother was born in, and hers before her? I was the first woman to leave our village, to come to America; the first woman who dared to achieve her dreams in New York."

Tears burn my eyelids as she recounts the few facts my father has always shared with me. "I—I thought there was a fire—"

My mother shakes her head, sadness drawn on her features. "There was never a fire. That's what your father told everyone—that I tried to set the house on fire while everyone was sleeping. It was a lie."

"So . . . you brought me into The Society for what . . . to help you get revenge on him?"

She doesn't answer, but her dark, expressive eyes tell me all I need to know.

"For all these years I thought . . . I . . . I thought my brain was *broken*. He made me believe that you and I are the same, that it was only a matter of time before mental illness swallowed me, took my life, made me . . . *unworthy*."

"He violated your trust, and I'm so sorry for that," Kat says. "The truth is that mental illness doesn't run in our family, Elyse. The truth is that your lineage is one of strong, smart women who stand up for what's right and good. Your grandmother and great-grandmother went against the grain in times when women were expected to obey, and that made them unpopular, especially among the men who were unfortunate enough to encounter them."

She continues: "The witch hysteria ripped through Slovenia just as it did the rest of Europe and America, and one of your ancestors was accused of witchcraft when she helped her cousin abort a pregnancy after she was raped by her husband. Your ancestor's name was Marija, and she was tortured and then drowned in the river alongside dozens of other women from our village. You know, men didn't burn witches, El—they burned *women*. Thinking, feeling, loving women, because they feared our intuitive power. I see you for who you really are, my precious daughter, I see the purity of your heart and the awareness in your eyes. The truth is that we *are* the same, you and I. And it's time to step into your birthright. Your *true* birthright, not the lies you've been told in an attempt to dim your light."

Aubrey's palm rests on my back, rubbing slow circles in a gesture of comfort. "I'm sorry you were fed so many lies. Our intention isn't to hurt you, but I know this must be hard to hear . . ."

Kat nods. "Justice is never straightforward. The abuse you've suffered runs deeper than you know, and the only way to reveal it to you was to show you. You never would have believed us if we'd just confessed everything from the beginning. Actions always speak louder than words, and taking back your power is a messy process that isn't without casualties."

"Do you believe us?" Aubrey whispers.

I blink once, twice, trying to let the truth settle in. I finally reply, "I believe you."

"So you understand?" Kat's eyes burn with promise. "Why what we do is important, why your next target makes sense?"

"I do." I nod.

"Perfect. I knew you were one of us." A slow smile lifts her lips. "Like mother, like daughter."

THIRTY-FOUR

Ellie

"What are you thinking?" Aubrey asks the moment we enter her apartment after leaving Kat's West Village townhome. I thought about going back to my own place, but the possibility of seeing Jack sets my blood on fire.

"I'm wondering if I married a monster, or if he became one the longer he worked for my dad."

"Both, maybe," muses Aubrey, who's wasted no time in pouring us each a glass of wine. "Evil runs through the heart of all of us; it just takes the right set of circumstances for it to show itself. Greed, power, money . . . name your poison."

"Optimistic." I can't help the snarky tone of my voice.

"Life is messy, dark, dangerous. And it's made all the worse when powerful people get away with despicable things."

"I wonder how many other secrets Jack's hiding. I wonder if he's ever had an affair," I say, thinking out loud.

Aubrey lets my question linger in the air before she finally replies, "Maybe. Men like him are used to getting what they want. Do you think he has?"

I think for a few long moments. "I don't think so. I think . . . maybe only after my emotional affair last year. That's when things really seemed to shift between us. He worked more; we talked less. Things fell apart." I sip my wine as I think about everything Jack and I have been through. "Have you ever been in love?"

"No." She swirls her wine, watching the red liquid coat the inside of the glass. "Honestly, I don't think I can be. I know it sounds weird, but I was raised in a home where love just wasn't a thing. Some people might call my mother neglectful, but I just think she was a pragmatic single mom. She put herself first always—there were no hugs or heartwarming after-school-special talks. I used to be so jealous of my friends who had loving families, but now I think my mom made me who I am—ruthless and calculating, but also strong and clever and controlled. I like who I am—maybe kids and a white picket fence aren't in my future, but I'm okay with that. I like being driven and commanding. You heard what Kat said about the women in her family: Men will take what you give them and run with it. I refuse to give any man any of me. I'll never have a real love story, but I'll also never know what I'm missing because I never had it to begin with. How could I miss something I've never experienced? I'm just not built for connecting like other people are. What about you?"

"I like being in love," I admit. "Even if it's the watered-down Disney version, I like having *my person* with me. It's nice being a family."

"Even if it's a false sense of family?" she asks, genuine curiosity sparking in her eyes.

"Well . . ." I frown as I consider her words. "Yes. I think so. Does that make me weak?"

"No, I don't think so." She smiles softly, nudging my shoulder with hers. "Naïve maybe, but not weak." Her gaze cuts away from mine, hovering out the window that overlooks 60th. "Do you think you'll divorce him?"

I take a deep breath. "Do you think I should?"

"I think it doesn't matter what I think. But . . ." She holds my gaze again. "If it were me . . . being the pessimistic and pragmatic girl I am . . . I think you catch more flies with honey, and I think the best way to get revenge is to keep your friends close and your enemies closer."

I nod, letting her words settle somewhere inside of me. "You're going to turn me into you, you know that?"

"Here's hoping." She giggles.

"I just can't shake the idea that he has more secrets hiding right under my nose," I confess. Warmth from the wine, and from our connection, hums through me. Aubrey may say she isn't capable of love or family, but for the first time I feel like I've found a sister—not just biologically, but in a real and supportive way. I can't explain why I've been so quick to trust her, but despite the fact that we're opposites in so many ways, I still feel a kinship with this woman.

"Maybe we should go all Nancy Drew on his ass." She laughs.

I chuckle. "Yeah?"

She nods, enthusiasm lighting up her green irises. "Let's conduct our own investigation. Starting in your apartment."

My eyes widen at her suggestion. "I already did do some searching—that's when I found the extra laptop and the security cameras and—"

"Ugh, of course he has security cameras. The bastard thinks he's entitled to so much power and access."

"I imagine he would say it's for safety—so I don't hurt myself."

"Well, how does that land now knowing that everything you've been told about your mental illness is a lie?"

"Is it, though?" I muse.

"Of course it is—everything Jack and your father said was meant to undermine your confidence and independence."

"But the bruises, the cutting, the sleepwalking—that's not made up," I say.

Aubrey doesn't answer. What can she say? There is no answer. I did do those things to myself—the evidence is embedded in my skin. I carry the scars of my self-harm as plain as day.

"Maybe it's the stress of being an abused woman that's caused it . . ." Aubrey finally says.

"Maybe," I say, but I don't believe her.

"Well, we won't know until we find out more about what Jack has been up to." She finishes her glass of wine and then stands from the sofa.

A minute later we're walking into my silent apartment. There's no sign that Jack has been here since I left early this morning, but that doesn't mean he isn't watching.

Waiting.

Ready to ruin me one poisoned arrow at a time.

THIRTY-FIVE

Aubrey

"This guy doesn't hang on to much," I comment as I flip through a stack of work files in Jack's home office. It isn't the first time I've been in here, but Ellie doesn't need to know that.

"He's a minimalist," Ellie confirms as she lifts another box from the closet.

"Minimalists aren't sentimental. I appreciate that," I say.

Ellie doesn't reply, just continues digging through another box. We've been at this for an hour. I'm not sure what we're looking for exactly, but I'm starting to think it isn't here.

"Hey—" I close the folder in my hand and toss it back onto the stack. I move across the room to settle beside Ellie on the floor. "Do you have access to his office downtown? Maybe he keeps the good stuff there."

Ellie considers. "No—maybe his secretary would let me in, but she would tell him."

"You don't think you could guess the passcode or find a key to get us in?"

"Maybe the passcode is the same as the laptop I found. I'm not sure." She's still digging through a box, distracted. "Wait!"

"Wait, what?" I lean closer.

"I've never seen this box before." Ellie's holding a gunmetal box that's engraved with Jack's initials.

"It looks like a gun case."

"Oh," she says. "Do you think . . ." She frowns, as if considering her next words.

"Do I think what?" I ask.

"Never mind." Ellie shakes her head, then flips the lock on the box and opens it. "What the fuck?"

"It's a phone . . ." I state the obvious.

Ellie powers on the smartphone, waiting for the screen to come to life. "I think I know what this is." As soon as the screen powers up she navigates to the messaging app. She opens it, then shakes her head when she finds the inbox empty. "Maybe I'm wrong."

"What did you think it was?" I ask.

"Those threatening messages I've been getting . . . I thought maybe it was him."

"Hm." I swipe the phone from her palm and then open the few apps that are on the home screen. Nothing interesting stands out to me beyond a few financial apps and one for mobile banking. "Wait—check this out." Ellie leans in when I open the contacts on the phone. "The only contact is you."

"Oh . . ." she breathes. "Do you think . . ."

"Do I think that he's been sending you threatening messages from this phone and deleting the evidence once he's finished?" I glance at her. "Maybe."

She nods then sighs. "I never thought . . . I don't understand why . . ."

"To undermine you and fuck with your sanity would be my guess," I say.

"So my own husband has been stalking me?" Anger flares in Ellie's voice.

"Maybe. I guess we don't have proof—"

"This is proof enough for me. What man has an extra phone? He's up to something, that's for sure. An affair, shady business deals, *something*." I've planted the seed that her husband might be a dishonest prick. "What am I supposed to do now?" Ellie asks.

"Well," I say, shoving the phone back in the box and closing the lid. "First things first: Did you turn off the security camera feed you found?"

"No, I didn't want to alert him that I know. He doesn't have a camera here in his office, though."

"Okay . . . good, so at least he doesn't know what we've found. Not yet anyway."

"Should I keep the phone? Throw it away? What's a woman supposed to do when she finds out her husband is keeping secrets?"

I hold Ellie's gaze for a few long beats, considering how to say my next words.

"I say we beat him at his own game."

"I don't know—I'm not good at playing games," Ellie says.

"Lucky for you, I am." A slow grin spreads across my face.

Ellie laughs awkwardly. "Should I be scared right now?"

"No—no, of course not." I push the metal box back into the cardboard one she found it in. "First we need to confirm he's been sending these messages."

"How?" Ellie asks.

"I bet my ex on the police force can get the call records to see what Jack has been up to on this phone. It might be a burner, but nothing is untraceable these days."

"And then what?" Ellie whispers.

"Well..." I arch an eyebrow. "Do you still have the milk and honey that were delivered from Westchester?"

Ellie frowns. "Yeah—why?"

"There's been a change of plans—I think we need to adapt," I say.

"What about Kat? Should we ask her what she thinks?"

I shake my head. "I think Kat would approve."

"Aubrey?" she says as we stand, shoving the box of Jack's secrets back in the closet.

"Yeah?" I say.

"What's in the honey and milk?"

I cross my arms and lean against the doorway to Jack's office. "I don't know for sure, but if I had to guess..." I pause, thinking through how much to reveal to Ellie. "Kat told you about the poisonous flowers in the Westchester garden, right?" Ellie nods, so I continue. "Well, bees that collect pollen from toxic flowers make toxic honey, if the percentage of toxic pollen is high enough. The same thing with cows that graze on toxic plants—it taints the milk."

"So... you think she wants me to poison my dad?" Ellie whispers.

I shrug. "Knowing her... yes."

I watch El's features as she processes the truth about the delivery from Westchester. All I can think is how trusting this woman is—how easily led. I'd resent her for her weakness, but I'd rather use it to my advantage. Ellie thinks she knows the truth, but the reality is that she'll never know the depths of her father and husband's corruption and depravity.

Not until the timing is right. Not until The Society is ready for her to know everything.

THIRTY-SIX

Ellie

The smell of smoke yanks me out of sleep.

I bolt upright, heart hammering against my ribs. For a moment, I don't know where I am. The couch digs into the back of my legs; the room swims before my eyes.

And then I hear it—a low, crackling hiss from the kitchen. The burners.

I stumble to my feet, dizzy, the heavy scent of gas stinging my nose and throat. I gag, coughing, and stagger toward the source. The stovetop is ablaze—one of the burners has caught fire, a greasy orange flame licking up toward the cabinets.

Panic claws at me.

I don't remember turning on the stove. I don't even remember lying down on the couch.

"Ellie!"

Jack's voice cuts through the haze. He bursts into the kitchen, barefoot, in sweatpants and a T-shirt, eyes wild. Without hesitation, he grabs the fire extinguisher from under the sink, rips the pin out, and blasts the fire with a shuddering spray of white foam.

It only takes a few seconds, but it feels like hours.

The flames die, leaving behind a scorched burner and a sickly chemical smell. The kitchen is a mess of soot and smoke. Jack tosses the extinguisher aside and grabs me by the shoulders.

"Jesus Christ, Ellie," he says. "What the hell happened?"

I can't answer.

Tears stream down my face without permission. My whole body shakes as if I'm standing outside in a blizzard.

"I—I don't know," I gasp. "I don't remember—"

He pulls me into his arms, clutching me tight against his chest. His T-shirt smells like laundry detergent and the faint, lingering scent of smoke. His heart pounds against my ear, fast and furious.

I sob into his shoulder, humiliated, terrified.

"I didn't—Jack, I swear—I didn't mean to—"

"Shh, it's okay, it's okay," he murmurs, stroking my hair. His hands are strong, anchoring. I want to believe this comfort is real, but something inside me coils tight, mistrusting.

"I don't remember turning anything on," I whisper, the words cracking apart in my throat. "I don't even remember getting off the couch—"

He leans back just enough to cup my face in his hands, wiping away tears with his thumbs. His expression is soft. Too soft. Like I'm a bomb about to detonate.

"You could have burned down the entire building, Ellie," he says, his voice low but sharp. "You could have killed yourself. Or someone else."

The words hit harder than any slap. I shrink under his gaze, the weight of guilt suffocating me.

"I'm sorry," I choke out. "I'm so sorry—"

Jack pulls me close again, kissing the top of my head. "It's not your fault, baby. It's the sickness. It's getting worse."

Sickness. The word rings in my ears like a death knell.

"I think..." He hesitates, rubbing slow circles into my back. "I think maybe it's time for something more serious. An inpatient program."

I stiffen against him. He feels it.

"You're not safe like this," he says, gentle but firm. "The therapy's not enough. You need real help, 24/7 care. Just for a little while."

A mental institution.

Like my mother.

I suck in a ragged breath, pulling back to look at him. His face is open, concerned, loving—and absolutely calculated.

I know it now. I know it in the marrow of my bones. This is what he's been working toward all along. Convincing me—and everyone else—that I'm dangerous. That I'm unstable. That I need to be locked away where no one will hear me scream.

"No," I whisper, but it's too weak, too automatic.

Jack smooths my hair back from my damp forehead. "Just for a little while. You'll get better. And when you come home, we'll be stronger than ever."

Home.

Stronger.

Better.

The lies are so sweet they almost lull me into nodding along. Almost.

But I remember the surveillance videos. The files.

I know what he really means.

If I disappear into an inpatient program, I'll never come back. Not as myself. Maybe not at all.

I bite down hard on the inside of my cheek to keep from shaking. I force myself to nod, just a little. Just enough.

"Maybe you're right," I whisper. "Maybe I need more help."

Relief crosses his face. He kisses my forehead again, lingering too long.

"I'll call Dr. Kessler in the morning," he murmurs. "She'll know what to do."

I nod again, mechanical. Hollow.

He thinks he's won. But what he doesn't know—what he can't even begin to imagine—is that I've already set the next trap.

And this time, he's the one who's never coming back.

THIRTY-SEVEN

Ellie

"Thanks for meeting me tonight for our anniversary dinner—it means a lot. I know things have been off between us lately—" Jack settles in his chair across from me at the Peninsula.

"Of course, I wouldn't miss it for the world." I send a saccharine smile across the table to Jack. I've been having flashbacks of the fire all day, confusion coiling in my stomach at the idea that I nearly burned my life to the ground—nearly lit the entire building and everyone in it on fire. I'm not sure if Jack has called Dr. Kessler yet—he hasn't said anything if he has, which leaves me more than a little on edge just waiting for the other shoe to drop.

"You're beautiful tonight. You always look beautiful, but this dress—is it new?" His gaze sweeps slowly over me.

"It is—thanks for noticing." I affect a look of genuine flattery. I have to act every part the sweet, doting wife if I'm going to play my hand well. I need him to trust me. I need him to believe that in my eyes, he can do no wrong. "Do you remember having one of our first dates here?"

"How could I forget? It was one of the best nights of my life." He reaches across the table to place a palm on mine. "Second only to our wedding night."

I smile, trying not to choke on the bile that's rising in my throat. "You're sweet."

"You are," he counters. "Work has been so hard lately, it feels like I'm barely keeping my head above water. You're the only bright spot, El—I hope you know that."

I don't reply because I don't think he wants me to. This is about him; this has always been about him. I need him to continue to believe that.

"I know I haven't been a good husband lately. I hope this night changes things, though. I did my best to re-create that date—the private rooftop dinner is just the start. I have a whole weekend planned for us."

"Oh?" I smile and thank the waiter when he arrives with a bottle of Veuve, filling our glasses with bubbles to the brim.

"To us." He holds his flute out and we say cheers. "At first I thought about a weekend upstate to celebrate, but that didn't feel good enough for my girl." I wait patiently for him to continue. "And then I thought maybe Cabo or—"

"Good evening," the waiter interrupts Jack. "Are we ready to order starters?"

Jack announces that we'll start with the tuna tartare. The waiter nods, then leaves. Jack starts to speak again, but as he does I reach for my glass and—seemingly by mistake—spill it across the table. My entire flute of champagne lands in his lap.

"Shit!" he cusses, reaching for his cloth napkin and dabbing at his slacks. "I'm going to clean this up in the bathroom. I'll be right back."

I apologize, but he waves me off.

As soon as he's gone, I pull out Jack's newly found burner phone from my bag and power it on. I open the messaging app and type in Jack's phone number. I shoot off a quick message.

If I can't have you, no one can.

The very same message as the last one he sent me.

A smile curves my lips as I tuck the phone back in my bag and pull out my own. I send Aubrey a quick message with a little winky face to let her know phase one of our plan has been set in motion. After Aubrey and I found Jack's burner phone two nights ago, we spent the next few hours orchestrating our next steps. She confirmed with her ex at the police department that Jack has been sending me the threatening messages from the anonymous number. That's all it took to convince me that I had to do something—that my husband couldn't be trusted.

By the time Jack returns, his face is pale and drawn. He's holding his phone in his hand—he hardly ever sets it down—so I know he saw my message.

"Everything okay?" I look up at him. "You look like you've seen a ghost."

"Ugh—yeah. Just . . . a work thing came up." He sits, setting his phone face down on the table.

"Oh, do you need to leave? We can raincheck if you need to."

"No—no, it's fine." He says he's fine, but I can see that he's distracted. A thrill of anticipation rises in me from knowing I've finally turned the tables on him. Taking back my power from a marriage that almost ruined me may be a process, but it's a fun one and it feels so good.

"I'm sorry I spilled on you," I offer. Jack just shakes his head, waving off my apology.

The waiter returns then with our tuna tartare, and we place our order for entrees. After enjoying a few bites of the tartare, I stand from the table and tell him I'm going to use the restroom. I leave the rooftop and move into the noisy main dining room.

Just as I reach the restrooms, I pause, realizing I left my bag at the table with Jack. If he suspects that I'm the one who sent the anonymous text message, he may dig through my bag and find the burner phone I used to send it. I turn, heading back in the direction of the table, but then I pause at the doors that lead out to the rooftop, watching as Jack cracks a small bottle open and pours a fine powder into my drink.

I blink once, twice, because I can't believe my eyes. Did he really just try to drug me? Without thinking, I push the heavy door open and stomp back to the table, crossing my arms when I reach it. "What the fuck was that?"

"Hey, baby—" He glances up at me.

"Don't *hey baby* me—what did you just put in my drink?"

"What are you talking about?" He looks up at me with kind, puppy dog eyes. I want to slap the unassuming look off his face.

"I saw you put something in my drink—"

His gaze turns dark and stormy. "You must be seeing things."

"Bullshit." I push his shoulder, then yank the cloth napkin off his lap. A small prescription bottle of pills falls to the floor at his feet. He moves to grab it but I beat him to it. "Ambien?" I read aloud. "Really?"

"I was worried." He spits it out. "If you'd just take care of yourself—"

I clamp my lips closed, not believing what's right in front of me. What's *always* been right in front of me. "How can I trust anything you say?"

He growls, gripping my wrist and pulling me closer to him. "Please don't make a scene."

"Easy for you to say—you're not the one being *drugged*."

"It's not like that. I was worried you weren't sleeping," he insists.

"Then you should have come home. You should have been there for me!"

He shakes his head. "You're right, I'm sorry." He feigns contrition. "Your dad's just been breathing down my neck lately, and I wanted to make sure you were getting a good night's sleep when I wasn't there."

"Where did you even get this prescription?" I ask, angrily shaking a handful of pills into my palm and then dumping them all into his flute of champagne.

"Your dad's personal physician."

"Fucking perfect. I should have figured he was in on it."

"He wasn't in on anything, El—"

"I don't believe you. I don't believe either one of you."

"What makes you say that?" He tips his head to the side.

"Nothing. Drink up, Jack. Go on, finish your glass."

"Stop it." He rolls his eyes.

"You know the effects Ambien can have on someone who doesn't need Ambien? Or someone who drinks while on it?" I seethe. He just shakes his head. "It can cause hallucinations, Jack. It can cause sleepwalking and lapses in memory and God knows what else!"

"It's fine, I was watching."

"Really? And just how were you watching from across town?" I dare him to tell me the truth—that he's been monitoring me via security cameras, but he remains silent. Coward.

"Why didn't you tell me you were this worried?" I let the smallest quiver of emotion lace my words.

"Because I . . . I didn't know . . . *how* to."

"So you drugged me instead, huh?" I watch him closely, looking for what, I'm not sure. Remorse? Regret? Resolve? "Oh my God—I just realized what this is really about."

"What? That I was trying to take care of you even when I couldn't be there?"

"Hardly." I flash him a sinister grin. "You were trying to control me. Trying to manufacture my instability, make me believe I was really having a psychotic break." I can't help the rage rising in my tone. "You did this! You made me crazy! You made me believe I couldn't even trust my own memories!" I stand from the table, shoving his flute of Ambien-laced Veuve Clicquot into his lap and throwing my napkin at him. "I hate you. I'm moving out. And if you get hit by a city bus on your way back downtown, don't think for a second that I'll be at the funeral. You deserve it."

And with that I walk out of the restaurant, my spine straight and my power regained. Kat was right—taking back my power is a process. I've spent all of my life tied to men who know only power and privilege. I have to be smart; I have to maneuver carefully or Jack will ruin me.

"Is everything okay, ma'am?" our server asks just as I reach the exit.

"Everything is fucking perfect." I give him a wicked smile. "Send another bottle of Veuve to the table, please. My husband needs it."

THIRTY-EIGHT

Ellie

The hotel room smells like fresh linen and lemon polish. The kind of cleanliness you can't get at home, no matter how hard you scrub. I sit cross-legged on the king-size bed, the duvet bunched up around me, Jack's laptop balanced on my thighs.

It's been two nights since I left Jack with champagne in his lap on the rooftop of the Peninsula during our anniversary dinner. I've been using my dad's credit card to pay for the most absurdly expensive hotel room at the Peninsula. Outside the window, Manhattan hums with horns, sirens, and life moving forward without me.

I should feel safe here. High up. Anonymous. Alone.

Instead, I feel flayed open. Raw. Betrayed.

The cursor blinks in the email I sent myself two nights ago. The attached files—hundreds of them, labeled by date and time—contain security footage pulled from the hidden system Jack tucked in vents and perched discreetly atop cupboards. The system he thought I'd never find.

I press play on the first clip.

It's me.

Sleeping.

For hours, nothing happens. I shift, murmur something in my sleep. The footage is grainy, cold, almost forensic. It feels like I'm watching a stranger.

Next clip: me getting ready for work. Pulling a dress over my head, towel-twisting my hair. Private moments stolen and archived without my knowledge.

Another clip: me in the kitchen, fumbling with a broken wine glass. A bright slash of blood blooms across my arm. I flinch as I remember that night—the phantom ache still present.

I click through hours of my life, feeling smaller with each file. Nothing unusual. Nothing criminal. Just the slow erosion of trust, dignity, self.

Maybe this was pointless. Maybe there's nothing here but a graveyard of my own humiliation. I'm about to close the window when a clip catches my eye—timestamped just over a week ago, 2:14 a.m.

I frown. I was asleep then.

I click play.

At first, I see the familiar layout of the living room: cream sofa, coffee table littered with Jack's whiskey tumblers, the soft halo of the lamp by the window.

And then—movement.

Jack.

And *Aubrey*.

At the door of the apartment.

Arguing.

My heart slams into my ribs. Aubrey's hair is pulled into a messy bun, her sweatshirt slipping from her shoulders. Jack is in jeans and a T-shirt, pacing like a caged animal.

I freeze the video and crank up the volume, but the microphone wasn't designed for this. Their voices are tinny, distorted. I catch fragments.

"You promised—" Aubrey hisses, stabbing a finger at Jack's chest.

"She wasn't supposed to find out!" Jack fires back, face twisted in a way I've never seen before.

"She's not stupid, Jack! She's starting to suspect—to remember!" Aubrey says, frantic. She grabs his sleeve, shaking him. "If she figures it out—if she pieces it together—"

Jack yanks his arm free. He glances toward the hallway—toward the bedroom. Toward me.

I'm there. Sleeping, just down the hall. Oblivious.

My stomach twists.

Aubrey's voice lowers, desperate. Almost pleading. "We have to end this."

Those five words ricochet around the hotel room, louder than any scream.

We have to end this.

The feed crackles. The footage blips, distorting into gray static. Gone. I stare at the frozen screen, my breath sawing in and out of my chest. They were in my home. Plotting. While I slept a few feet away.

Aubrey—the friend—my sister—who held my hand when I thought Jack was pulling away.

And Jack—my husband. My betrayer. My jailer.

My mind races, sifting through the hundreds of conversations Aubrey and I shared over coffee, wine, endless afternoons spent pretending everything was normal. Had she been studying me? Reporting back?

Had Jack been pulling the strings the whole time, or had Aubrey joined him willingly?

How deep does it go? And what exactly do they think I'm starting to suspect?

I dig my nails into the duvet, grounding myself. *Think, Ellie. Think.*

The strange gaps in my memory. The sleepwalking episodes. The overwhelming sense that someone was always watching.

Maybe I wasn't crazy. Maybe I wasn't breaking.

Maybe they were making me believe I was.

My gaze flicks to the laptop again. There are more videos. Dozens I haven't opened yet. I swallow hard, suddenly afraid of what else I might find. More proof of their lies? Evidence of something worse?

Aubrey said *She's starting to suspect—to remember.*

What did they make me forget?

I scroll back through the folder, looking for another clip around the same date, desperate for more context. But the videos jump hours ahead, as if the feed was deliberately cut.

Deleted. Erased.

But not before I found that sliver. Not before they revealed themselves.

I sit back against the headboard, cradling the laptop like it's a bomb wired to my heartbeat. They want me to doubt myself. They want me to lose track of what's real. That's the weapon. Not force. Not bullets. *Doubt.*

I'm not playing their game anymore.

I click into a secure cloud account I set up a few days ago, back when adrenaline and fear first shoved me out the door and into this hotel. I upload the video—the damning clip of Jack and Aubrey in my apartment—to the drive.

Insurance.

Because if they come for me, if they try to bury me under another layer of lies, I'll bury them first.

A cold, steady resolve coils in my chest. They think they can erase me. They have no idea who they're dealing with. Not anymore.

THIRTY-NINE

Ellie

The security code hasn't changed.

That's the first thing I notice when the keypad beeps under my fingertips and the heavy front door of my father's penthouse clicks open. I don't hesitate—just slip inside, closing the door behind me as quietly as I can.

The penthouse is exactly as I remember it: cold, cavernous, painfully curated. Every surface gleams, from the black marble floors to the chrome and glass furniture. It smells faintly of cedar and something sharper—money, maybe, if money had a scent.

I move fast. I know my father's routine; I know he won't be back until after seven—if he comes home at all.

The first floor yields nothing—just the same sterile living room, the massive empty kitchen, the closed-off study. I search anyway, brushing my fingers over the bookshelves, the locked liquor cabinets. Everything staged, everything hollow.

It's only when I reach the back hallway, the one leading to the old servants' quarters, that my pulse spikes. Growing up, my father always kept the door to the hallway locked, claiming the servants' quarters was just for storage. I'd never questioned it.

Now, the door is cracked open. I slip inside.

The air smells stale, untouched. Dust motes spiral in the shafts of afternoon light slipping through narrow, high windows. The cramped hallway leads to a small, bare room—and inside, chaos.

Boxes stacked floor to ceiling. Folders spilling their contents across the floor. A battered metal filing cabinet with drawers half-open. I step closer.

The first box I check is filled with thick manila folders stamped with the seal of Greystone Psychiatric—the facility where my father said my mother died.

I pull out a file and flip it open.

Subject: Valeria Thomas. Diagnosis: Acute Delusional Disorder. Paranoia. Emotional Instability. Violent Tendencies.

Page after page of medical jargon. Incident reports. Psychiatric evaluations. Redacted sections so heavy with black ink the pages look burned.

I dig deeper. Another box, filled with surveillance photos—of me.

Me at five years old, holding a popsicle in the park. Me at seven, walking into my elementary school. Me at ten, sitting alone at the edge of a soccer field.

All dated. All cataloged. As if I were a specimen under observation. My stomach twists.

I rifle through the folders, heart pounding harder with every discovery. Some of the files detail treatments for my mother approved by my father—sedatives prescribed without my mother's consent. There are notes about her "declining cooperation." Recommendations for "permanent solutions."

Permanent solutions.

I press my knuckles against my mouth, willing down the nausea rising in my throat.

My father didn't just commit my mother.

He orchestrated her erasure.

I shove the files into my bag, my hands shaking. There's something else gnawing at the edges of my mind. Something more.

The closet door at the back of the servants' room is slightly ajar. I cross the room in two steps and tug it open fully. Inside: nothing but a dusty floor, peeling walls, and a loose floorboard. My breath catches.

I drop to my knees and wedge my fingers under the edge of the plank, prying it up. Dust fills my nose, making my eyes water.

Beneath the floorboard lies a single battered object: a leather journal, the spine cracked and the corners worn soft with time. I lift it out carefully, like it might fall apart in my hands. The name scrawled inside the front cover makes my heart break: **Valeria Thomas.**

I sit back against the wall and crack it open, flipping past the first few empty pages until the inked words begin, messy and desperate.

April 17

> *I don't know who to trust anymore. I hear them at night—the clicks on the phone line, the whispers behind closed doors. Even when I'm smiling at the charity luncheons, they're watching me.*

May 2

> *Daniel says I'm imagining things. That I'm stressed. That I need a rest. He's started suggesting*

medication. *"Just to help,"* he says. *Help with what? Forgetting?*

May 19

My mother was right. Men like him—men of power, of greed, of privilege—they don't love like we do. Love isn't love to them. It's ownership. A means to an end. She warned me before the wedding. I didn't listen.

June 4

I think he's setting me up. Gaslighting me. Things go missing: my jewelry, letters, my birth control pills. When I ask, he laughs and kisses my forehead and tells me I must have misplaced them. I can't breathe sometimes, like the walls are closing in. I feel trapped in this golden cage he built. And I can't tell anyone. Because who would ever believe me over him?

I want to stop reading, but I don't stop. I can't.

Entry after entry paints a picture not of a deranged woman, but of a woman being systematically broken down. Stripped of her autonomy. Isolated. Made to doubt her own reality.

Exactly what Jack—and Aubrey—are doing to me now.

The final entries grow more erratic, the handwriting sharp and jagged.

July 11

He said if I keep causing problems, he'll make sure I'm taken care of. Forever. I think he means it. I have to find a way out. For me. For Ellie. She's still young enough. She can forget.

July 14

> *He threatened me today. Said he'd tell everyone I was unstable. That he'd show them the records. What records? I never consented to anything. If you find this, Ellie—don't trust him. Don't trust any of them.*

The journal ends there. No final farewell. No explanation. Just a warning.

I clutch the journal against my chest, the dusty air rasping in my lungs. My mother wasn't crazy. She was trapped. Controlled. Destroyed. By the very people who claimed to love her.

Just like me.

I jam the journal into my tote bag and replace the floorboard, leaving no sign I was here. I have to get out before my father comes back. Before he realizes what I've found. A thousand thoughts charge through my mind, but one screams louder than all the rest:

If they did it to her, they'll do it to me.

Unless I end this first. My heart hammers against my ribs. I need to leave. Now. Every instinct screams it. But something stops me.

On a low shelf near the closet's back wall, half-buried under yellowing papers and dusty storage boxes, a small wooden jewelry box with a pearl inlay catches my eye. A strip of metal with tarnished gold lettering curls off the lid, but I can still make out the initials: **V.T.**

Valeria Thomas.

My mother's jewelry box.

Hands trembling, I pull it free and flip open the clasp. A soft, mechanical whirring fills the air. And then—music.

A crackling, broken version of "Clair de Lune" lilts into the empty room, so distorted it sounds like it's playing underwater. A tiny, cracked prima ballerina pops upright, spinning stiffly on one worn slipper, her porcelain face frozen in a blissful, eerie smile.

The sound hits me like a punch. Suddenly, I'm not in the servants' quarters anymore.

I'm five years old, peeking out from behind the heavy velvet drapes in the penthouse living room. The sunlight catches the gleaming marble, casting long shadows across the floor. The music box is open on the side table, playing the same broken melody. I remember clutching my stuffed rabbit, thumb tucked between my teeth, heart pounding against my tiny chest.

And then—chaos.

Men in white coats storm into the room, moving too fast, too loud. I hear my mother scream—a raw, panicked sound that makes the hairs on my arms stand up even now.

They grab her roughly by the arms. She thrashes, kicking over a vase, sending shards skittering across the floor. I remember the sickening crash. The way she twisted and fought like a trapped animal.

And my father standing by the fireplace, stone-faced. Watching.

He doesn't move. He doesn't stop them.

He *lets it happen.*

My mother turns her head sharply, wild-eyed, hair loose around her face. She finds me—my small, hidden form behind the curtains—and our eyes lock.

"Don't believe him!" she screams.

The words are so sharp, so loud, they cut through everything—the men's shouts, the shattered glass, the music box's haunting, broken song.

And then she's gone, dragged out the front door. The lock clicks shut behind them.

I stand frozen, the music box playing its last, desperate notes. My father kneels beside me, calm and steady, brushing my hair back from my face. His voice smooth and warm.

"She's sick, Ellie," he whispers. "She had to go away. But don't worry. Daddy's here. I'll take care of you."

He pulls me into a hug, wrapping me up in his arms. I remember his suit smelled like cold air and cologne. I remember wanting to pull away but being too afraid. Because even at five years old, I knew my mother was right: He was lying.

The music box sputters to silence in the present. I sit there on the dusty floor, shaking, the velvet box still open in my lap, the little ballerina slowly winding down, her dance jerky and incomplete. My skin is clammy. My stomach churns. I wasn't wrong about my mother. I wasn't wrong about any of it.

He made me forget. He *trained* me to forget. Rewrote my memories with bedtime stories and empty promises and polished smiles. He buried my mother alive in some psychiatric facility.

And then he buried the truth.

I slam the jewelry box shut. It feels violent. I need to get out of here before he comes back. I push to my feet, dizzy, my legs cramping from sitting so long. I tuck the box into my bag next to the journal, zip the bag shut, and sling it over my shoulder.

As I move toward the door, I catch my reflection in the cracked mirror hanging next to the door.

I barely recognize myself. My hair is wild, face flushed, eyes wide with something between terror and rage. I vow then to stop doubting myself. No more listening to their lies.

Jack. Aubrey. My father. All of them.

They think they're playing me. They think I'm still the girl they gaslit into silence. But they forgot something. They forgot whose blood runs in my veins.

My mother's.

Like mother, like daughter. Kat's words ring in my mind.

And she fought tooth and nail.

Now it's my turn.

FORTY

Ellie

Fifteen minutes later I step into my apartment, my mind set on getting Jack's backup laptop as quickly as I can. I need to dig a little deeper into the financial affairs Jack's been keeping from me before I confront him about any of it. The apartment is quiet, untouched. I miss it. My heart clenches with the desire to just go back to *before*. Before everything got complicated and I realized that nothing in my life is what it seems. I set my bag down on the side table and move in the direction of Jack's office when I hear it.

"Babe—" A feminine giggle echoes down my hallway.

I turn my head just in time to see my husband come around the corner. Aubrey trails after him wearing just a lacy bra and thong underwear.

"Oh my God." They both whip around at my words. Jack's face falls like he's seen a ghost. Aubrey tries to cover herself with my husband's body, but the damage is already done.

"E-El—" Jack stammers but remains frozen.

"Are you okay?" Aubrey's eyes hang heavy on mine, almost like she's genuinely concerned.

"I was until you walked out with my husband looking like that," I snap. Aubrey opens her mouth and then closes it again, like a fish gasping for air. I lean a hip against the table, crossing my arms and then letting a dark smile cross my face.

"I can explain, El—" Jack begins.

"I doubt that."

Jack's eyes hang heavy with mine. The silence throbs like a heartbeat between us.

"This isn't what it looks like, El—" Aubrey begins. I cut my cold gaze to hers. "Just hear me out—I promise it will all make sense."

"No. No it won't." A growl that's practically feral leaves my lips. "I had a feeling after I saw you both at the Peninsula the other night—"

"No—" Aubrey interrupts me.

"Get out." I seethe. "Both of you, get the fuck out of my life."

"El—it's not that simple."

"It is. I can't look at either of you right now." My heart hammers wildly. "Everything suddenly makes so much more sense."

"Does it?" Jack asks.

I bite down on my bottom lip to stop myself from crying. "How long has this been going on?"

Jack shakes his head, words caught in his throat. Aubrey glances down at the floor, shame blossoming crimson on her cheeks. "Perfect, just fucking perfect," I say to Jack. "You carry on right under my nose for who knows how long, and then you're too much of a fucking coward to tell me how long you've been playing me?"

My rage reaches a fever pitch and I throw the nearest thing within distance at his head. One of the engraved pens my father gave to employees as Christmas gifts last year whips across the room. My aim is bad, so it bounces off the fridge just above his head. He ducks anyway, cringes, and then latches onto Aubrey's hand and drags her down the hallway.

"Get out of my house!" I shriek after them. I feel like a fool. I should have listened to my instincts and confronted them the other night at the Peninsula, but then, what good would that have done?

I'm still shaking with rage when Aubrey slinks out of my front door a minute later, refusing to even look at me. Jack returns to the kitchen as soon as Aubrey's left.

"Please, will you let me explain? Let's just be rational about this, El."

"Fine. You can start by explaining why my dad is paying you all of this money from an offshore account."

Jack's gaze falls to the file clutched in my hand. "Oh, you noticed that?"

"Sure did." I widen my eyes, challenging him to try to explain this.

"I was helping your dad with a sensitive case," he says, taking a few steps forward.

"Don't—stay right there. Don't come any closer." I hold up a hand.

"El—"

"Don't *El* me." I mock him. "Tell me the truth or I'm filing for divorce first thing in the morning."

"El—"

"Stop it! Just be honest with me for once, would you?"

He frowns, moves to take a step toward me, then seems to think better of it and pauses. "When I was an intern at your dad's company—"

"In college?" I ask, disbelief crowding my thoughts.

"In college," he continues. "I witnessed something that would have ruined all of us. Him, me, you, all of Northrup Thomas." I don't say anything because there isn't anything to say. I start thinking back on the more than ten years since that time—was anything real? "Your dad didn't trust anyone else, so I helped him *handle* things."

"Handle things, huh? That doesn't sound good." I think about the check stubs and the giant amounts of money that have been flowing back and forth between my dad and Jack. "One of the check stubs in the file is dated from last month."

Jack nods. I can almost see the thoughts running through his head. "That summer I was an intern at Northrup Thomas was just the beginning."

"That's the summer before we met."

Jack nods, his silence confirming all of my worst fears.

"You—you only started dating me because I'm my father's daughter, right? Did he put you up to it?"

"What? To marrying you?" Jack is shifting back and forth, uncomfortable with my scrutiny. "Of course not."

"Of course not. *Right*," I snap. "I can't trust anything that comes out of your mouth."

"You can, El. You're the only thing I think about from the moment I wake up until I fall asleep at night. Everything I do is for you."

"Liar. You don't even come home most nights." I think of all the nights he must've spent with Aubrey—and maybe she's only one in a line of affairs he's had right under my nose. "Is that why you moved her in right next to me? To babysit me?"

"That's insane—of course not."

"Is it?" I snap. "Seems like the most obvious setup to me."

"Aubrey and I just met—"

"Bullshit!" I scream.

"I swear."

"And you didn't marry me because of my dad? And you didn't start taking all of this money from him as a payment for marrying me? Like a fucking dowry or some bullshit."

"El—that's crazy." Jack approaches me with an arm extended. "I love you."

"You have a funny way of showing it." I shove stacks of his work files and folders off the kitchen island, and they fly in a tornado of chaos, landing across our kitchen and dining room floor. "I hate you."

"No—fuck—please, just hear me out."

"I can't," I admit, shaking my head. It's so tiring hating someone you love.

I go into our bedroom, closing the door behind me as tears flood my eyes. I settle on my bed, thinking I may never have the energy to leave this room again. What kind of secrets could possibly be worth the hundreds of thousands of dollars my dad has been shuttling into accounts in my husband's name?

Investments? Money laundering? *Murder?*

I can't stand to look at my husband's face—not now, maybe never again.

FORTY-ONE

Ellie

I've been camped out at the hotel for a week since the confrontation with Jack and Aubrey in my apartment. I was just starting to wrap my head around the idea that my husband has been money laundering on behalf of my father to banks in the Caymans, or handling some other less-than-ethical businesses for him, but now this?

I've been working from the hotel bed every day, rescheduling all meetings and calls and handling only the most pressing matters. Eating has been nearly impossible, but out of sheer will, I've ordered room service, even though it mostly goes untouched. My mind keeps replaying the moment Aubrey walked out in her underwear, her hands on my husband's skin. His easy smile that I haven't seen in months, not since I messed up and had my own extramarital... *whatever* with Jason. To escape my thoughts, I've forced myself out of the hotel for some fresh air.

Walking in Central Park feels like just the kind of refresh I need, but as I pass one of the fountains my mind is drawn back to a day years ago with Jack, right after my graduation at Columbia.

The sun is warm on my cheeks, golden and perfect. Columbia's lawn buzzes with laughter, clinking champagne glasses, and the flash of cameras. I'm still clutching my diploma with both hands, afraid that if I blink, I'll wake up and find this whole day was a dream.

But then Jack touches my arm and everything sharpens into focus.

He's smiling—wide, boyish, that kind of grin that makes you forget your name. "Come here," he says, guiding me away from the crowd with a hand on my back. "Just for a second."

I laugh. "Jack, where are we going? I'm supposed to meet my dad at the photo tent—"

But then he stops walking. And drops to one knee. The world quiets. I hear someone gasp. Maybe me.

"Ellie." He looks up at me with those impossibly brown eyes. That charming, disarming smile.

"We've only been together six months," he says, loud enough for the crowd gathering to hear. "But when you know ... you know. Right?"

My breath catches.

"I knew the first time you rolled your eyes at me during that guest lecture," he continues, making the small group around us chuckle. "You were so sharp, so beautiful, so completely uninterested in being impressed."

I cover my mouth with my hand. He pulls a tiny velvet box from his pocket. Opens it. The diamond catches the sun like a spark. "I knew I'd spend the rest of my life chasing that spark," he says. "If you'll let me."

A pause. The whole commons is silent now.

"Elyse Valentinja Thomas," he says, voice steady, "will you marry me?"

The breath whooshes out of me. Tears sting my eyes before I can stop them. "Yes," I whisper. Then louder, with a watery laugh: "Yes."

The crowd erupts in cheers. A group of undergrads whistles and applauds. Jack stands, slips the ring onto my shaking finger, and pulls me into his arms. We're both laughing, crying, kissing through it. And then—

"My baby girl!" My father barrels through the crowd, arms wide, eyes glassy with tears. He hugs us both, tight and proud. "I can't believe it," he says, voice thick. "I mean, I can—I've known for a while— but still. You found your forever, Ellie." He squeezes my shoulder. "And, Jack . . . you're the only man I'd ever trust with taking care of her."

Jack gives him a grateful nod, pulling me in tighter.

"I'll protect her with my life," he says, and somehow, in this moment, I believe him.

My heart feels too full, stretched at the seams.

I look down at the ring. Then at Jack. Then at my father. Two strong men. Two great loves. And I think—how did I get so lucky?

The lawn blurs around me. The world spins in soft, perfect colors. Today is everything. Today is the beginning of forever. And I've never felt more loved.

I settle at the edge of the bubbling water, letting the sunshine warm my face. I lie down on the pink granite wall that surrounds the fountain and try to calm my racing mind for the first time in a week.

"El—" My husband's voice cuts through my peace. "It's about time you left that fucking hotel. I've been emailing, calling, texting—"

"Ugh—what—are you following me now? I blocked you for a reason, Jack," I say, not even bothering to open my eyes. Maybe if I ignore him, he'll go away.

"Please, just hear me out for a minute. There's so much you don't know."

"Oh, I'm aware. I know this may come as a shock, but I don't want to know anymore, Jack. I really don't. Take a hint."

"I can't. I won't. You're my wife, El, please just hear me out."

I don't reply. I don't want to hear him out, but I also don't have the words to fight him anymore. The truth is I never did, and maybe that's why I gave in to him so easily over the course of our marriage. I thought I could trust him to be in charge, but that may be my greatest error of all of them over the years.

"I know you met with Kat—your real mother—but you don't know the whole story." I sense him sit down next to me. My heart clatters in my ears as I wait for him to continue. "She's not the noble matriarch she may have you believe." I still don't reply, so he continues, "In fact, she's more a manipulative gold digger hell-bent on revenge than she is anything else."

"According to who? *You?* My father?"

He sighs, "El—"

I push myself up to sitting and turn to face the man I vowed to love. "You were drugging me! Please, just cut the condescending bullshit."

"I am," he barks. "Just let me tell you a story, then you can make an informed decision."

I hold his gaze, giving him my best poker face. "You have five minutes."

He groans and rolls his eyes, but then seems to catch himself. "Fine. Have it your way. Your mother married your father for power, not love. She came to America as a poor immigrant and orchestrated her climb to the top—"

"Yeah, I think it's called the American Dream—"

"Well, most American Dreams don't involve murder, do they?"

"I'm sure plenty of them do—we just don't get the seedy side of the story in the history books," I shoot back.

"It's noble to think that your mother was an abused wife—that she discovered your dad's true nature and then set The Society against him—but that's only one side of the story. The truth is she's been tracking and eliminating powerful men for years—long before she even married your dad, Ellie." He frowns, dark eyes clinging to mine. "Your mother is a serial killer of men."

FORTY-TWO

Ellie

"You're insane," I tell him, gathering my bag to head back to the hotel.

"Am I, Ellie? Really?" He sits on the edge of the fountain for a long moment, his hands clasped in his lap. He looks contrite for the first time in years—maybe ever. "The fact is, I don't have any proof to show you, but surely you've realized you don't have any proof to discredit me either."

I clamp my lips closed because he's right.

"Your father outmaneuvered your mother once he realized what her game was. He convinced the world she was insane to protect himself and you." His gaze penetrates mine. I feel like I'm in the spotlight, like he's asking more of me than I have to give.

"So what am I supposed to think about finding Aubrey nearly naked and wrapped around you in our apartment?"

"I know it looks bad, but it wasn't. Listen, I swear to you nothing happened between us. She stopped over to drop off mail that was delivered to the wrong address and I spilled all over her so I offered a change of clothes."

"Right," I utter, not believing a word.

"Do you believe me?" he finally asks.

I weigh my options, Aubrey's comment long ago about keeping my friends close and my enemies closer ringing through my mind. I swallow my pride and allow the lie to leave my lips. "Yes, I believe you."

Now is the time to end this for good, I think. A new chapter is waiting—I can't stay stuck in neutral forever, and I can't let my husband know I suspect him of far bigger crimes than this one.

"Good." Jack sighs with relief. He stands, holding his arms out for a hug. "Thank you for giving me a minute to explain."

I nod, then stand and allow him to wrap me in his once-comforting embrace. He plants a kiss on the crown of my head and whispers, "Please, come home."

I remain silent, unwilling to give him anything else.

"Please, El—" His palms press harder into my back. Maybe it's in an effort to comfort me, but I can't help but feel suffocated and controlled. "I forgave you for your indiscretion last year—let's just put all of this behind us and move on. Together."

I nod against his chest, sobs forming painfully in my throat. "Okay. I think I'd like to try again—to rebuild."

Relief floods Jack's tense muscles, and he loosens his grip on me, placing one last kiss on my forehead before pulling away. "Thank God. Fuck, I haven't slept in a week thinking I'd lost you for good."

I don't respond. Let him think what he wants, but the truth remains that he has lost me. I'm just not ready for him to know that yet. I still have work to do here.

FORTY-THREE

Aubrey

The skyline glitters beyond the floor-to-ceiling glass like a graveyard of dying stars. Jack's office is too clean, too polished, the kind of place built for men who make their living hiding rot beneath marble and leather. I sit on the edge of his desk, legs crossed, watching him pour himself a drink he doesn't need.

He's quiet for a moment too long. I hate when he does that—when he tries to look thoughtful. It never suits him.

"She's coming back," he finally says, voice low.

I blink once. "Excuse me?"

"Ellie. We talked yesterday. She's moving back in."

I laugh—sharp and quick, like glass cracking under pressure. "You're kidding."

He doesn't look up from the ice swirling in his glass. "She said she forgives me."

"Well, that makes one of us."

Jack sighs and takes a sip. "She wants to try again. To rebuild. She said maybe she hadn't been giving enough. That she understands why I—why *we*—happened."

"That woman couldn't 'give enough' if she came with a bow and a receipt," I snap. "Jesus, Jack. You had your tongue halfway down my throat two nights ago, and now she's back in your bed like it never happened?"

He flinches. Just a flicker, but I see it.

"She caught us," I continue. "She saw. And she still came crawling home? Do you hear yourself?"

"She's been . . . vulnerable," he says, softer now. "This year's been hard on her. I can't just throw her away."

"You don't have to throw her away." I lean in, smile slow and cruel. "You already broke her."

Jack sets his drink down too carefully, the kind of control that reeks of guilt.

"You're not seeing the full picture," he says. "We have to be more careful now. No more hotel rooms. No more surprise visits to the apartment. She's watching everything."

I arch a brow. "Really?"

Jack doesn't respond.

"Look," I say, sliding off the desk and smoothing my skirt. "Ellie's not dangerous. She's weak. A spineless little rabbit who wants so badly to be loved, she'll swallow any betrayal if it means someone holds her hand after."

Jack shakes his head. "You don't know her like I do."

"Please." I roll my eyes. "I've known her longer than you have. I know the type. You give her a false sense of safety, and she'll cling to it like a child clings to a burning blanket. She came back once, Jack. That's proof she'll always come back. You can do anything you want now."

He looks at me then. Really looks. Like he's trying to decide if I'm the devil or the only one who sees clearly.

I smile. "She gave you permission to take whatever you want. Now you don't have to worry about repercussions. Not from her."

Jack presses his fingers to his temples. "You make it sound so . . . calculated."

"It is." I step closer. "That's the point. You're not a boy, Jack. You don't stumble into affairs. You build them. You mold the story you need to survive."

His hands drop to his sides. He looks tired. Haunted.

"I don't feel good about it," he says. "None of it. Lying to her, manipulating her, watching her unravel because of us . . . I didn't mean to go this far. But I can't dig my way out if I tried. I'm already buried. And there are people involved—very powerful people—who won't let me back out now."

I touch his chest gently, then trail my hand to his shoulder, thinking about all the secrets this man has told me under the guise of pillow talk. "You're not getting out, Jack. Not because they won't let you . . . but because you don't want to. You want to win. You always have."

He exhales like he's trying not to collapse under the weight of it all.

I slide my arms around him, press my body against his. He lets me.

"You did what you had to do," I murmur against his ear. "You made the choices no one else had the stomach to make."

His hands close around my waist. He leans into me like a man on the edge of a cliff. I lower my voice, right into his ear. "Vanquishing evil isn't pretty, Jack. Sometimes there's collateral damage. But it's worth it in the end."

He doesn't respond. But he doesn't pull away either. And that's all I need.

FORTY-FOUR

Ellie

The laptop is exactly where I found it last time—hidden inside a small black safe on the bookshelf. If I didn't already know to look for it, I'd have missed it again.

But I know Jack now.

I know where he hides the truth.

I carry the laptop to the dining table, fingers trembling as I plug it in. The screen flickers to life. The desktop is bare, sterile. A single folder sits in the corner labeled simply: *ARCHIVE*.

I open it.

Inside are dozens of subfolders—each labeled with dates, timestamps, and generic location titles: *Living Room Cam, Kitchen Feed, Bedroom 2*.

I click on one marked *07-16_Kitchen_2AM*.

The video loads slowly, and then I see it: my kitchen, dark and quiet. I'm there, barely visible in the corner of the frame, curled on the couch, motionless. Sound asleep.

The camera doesn't move. But Jack does.

He walks into frame at 2:17 a.m., barefoot, in a T-shirt and pajama pants. He moves with purpose—turns each burner on one by one.

He opens the cabinet, takes something out. A rag. He dips it in a bottle of alcohol and leaves it precariously near the flame. I watch, horrified, as he stands for a moment, gazing at the flickering gas blue beneath the pan like he's admiring a painting. Then he walks over to the couch—to me—and gently lifts my head to place a pillow beneath it.

He brushes the hair from my face. Soft. Loving. A performance.

Then he walks out of frame.

Ten minutes later, the fire starts.

I slam the laptop shut so hard the click echoes through the room.

My heart pounds, not from fear—but from rage.

He did it. He set the fire. While I slept.

He wanted the chaos, the smoke, the confusion. He wanted me to wake up shaking, afraid of my own hands, convinced that I'd nearly burned down our home.

It worked.

I cried in his arms. I believed him when he said I needed help. I swallowed the pills he gave me. *Just to help you sleep, sweetheart. You're not yourself.*

I *was* myself. I was the only real thing in the whole damn apartment. Jack just drugged that version of me into silence. Because he needed a sweet, simpering wife at home.

He wanted the best of both worlds. Me: the pristine wife. Aubrey: the uninhibited escape.

And all the power and profit of my father's empire, untouched by suspicion. He's a master of compartmentalization. Every part of his life in its place.

Until now.

Until *me*.

I pace the kitchen—our kitchen—and suddenly the space feels unfamiliar. Cold. This was never my home. It was a stage set. A carefully curated illusion where I played the role he cast me in.

But I've read the script now.

And I'm rewriting the ending.

I return to the laptop, open the folder again. I watch him do it three more times—small manipulations caught on silent, grainy video. Planting the gun in the sink. Drugging my orange juice before bringing me breakfast in bed. Deleting files from my phone while I sleep. All while telling me that I'm just "overwhelmed."

Every time I doubted myself, Jack was there to confirm that I should. Every time I questioned him, he said I was tired, hormonal, or unstable.

No. I wasn't broken. I was *being* broken.

On purpose.

And now that I see it, I can't unsee it. I grab a legal pad from the drawer and begin to write. Not notes—a plan. Not just to leave. Not just to survive. To ruin him.

I have the footage. I have the financial contracts. I have the bank account numbers he never thought I'd find. And now, I have something more powerful than all of that: clarity.

A manipulator. A fraud. Maybe even evil. But I see it now—I see him clearly. And I see myself clearly too. Not the victim he wanted me to become. Not the wife who smiles through betrayal. Not the woman who doubts her own mind.

I hold every key to destroy him.

All I have to do is *turn the lock*.

I sit down, set the phone on the table, take a breath, and press record. My voice is calm, steady.

"This is my statement," I begin. "My name is Elyse Valentinja Taylor, and if you're hearing this, I've already exposed Jack Taylor, alias Julian McCallister, and the crimes he's committed."

I smile as the green light shows at the top of the screen indicating that the mic is in use. Because now, I'm not just surviving his story.

I'm *writing my own*. And this time—he's the one who won't see it coming.

The phone buzzes against the table.

My hands are still shaking from watching Jack set the fire, drugging me over the weeks and months, planting the gun in the sink—watching him *tuck me in* after lighting the burners, as if that somehow absolved him. I glance at the screen, expecting another meaningless notification. Instead, it's a message from an unknown number.

We finish this, together. Like mother, like daughter . . .

I stare at the text, reading it once, then twice more. The room shifts around me. Not with fear. With clarity. She knows. She's watching too. Not just Jack. My mother.

The woman I thought had died in a psychiatric hospital when I was seven. The woman I thought had been broken by my father, locked away and left to rot. But now I know the truth—she didn't die. She disappeared. And she's been *waiting*.

My mind scrambles to find comfort in the words. *Together* sounds good. *Mother* sounds like salvation.

But I don't trust that voice anymore.

My mother didn't send this message because she wants to save me. She sent it because she sees herself in me—because we're two sides of the same blade. And I don't know which one of us is sharper.

I grip the edge of the table to steady myself. The message is a warning disguised as comfort.

I can't trust her. I can't trust *either* of them.

I turn back to the laptop. The grainy image of the kitchen burner hissing to life stares back at me. Jack's figure moves like a shadow on a stage. He's a monster in plain sight now.

I click through the folder, reopen the surveillance system. Live feeds begin to flicker to life across the screen—bedroom, hallway, balcony. They've been watching *me* all along.

Well, now I'm watching *him*. I click a few keys and activate the mirroring program I found via a quick internet search. Every feed is now also streaming to the encrypted drive I control. Not Jack. Not my mother. Me.

Then I open the dummy email I created under an alias—L.Grey_Archive—and attach the fire and other incriminating footage and a few select financial documents. I type one sentence into the draft subject line: **This is just the beginning.**

Then I save it to drafts. Not sent. Not yet. A loaded weapon waiting for the right time to pull the trigger. I sit back in the chair and breathe slowly. The plan is already in motion.

Jack thinks I'm broken. My mother thinks I'm hers. My father thinks I'm irrelevant.

They're all wrong.

FORTY-FIVE

Ellie

I pace the apartment barefoot, the hem of my robe dragging over the polished hardwood. The curtains are half-drawn, just enough to let the evening light slant in, casting long distorted shadows.

I know he's watching.

The thought prickles the back of my neck, but I keep my performance steady. I let my fingers twitch at my sides like I can't control them. I mutter under my breath, snatches of nonsense, fractured conversations with ghosts that aren't there.

"Stop it, stop it, stop it," I whisper, tugging at the ends of my hair. "It's not real. It's not—" I cut myself off with a sharp laugh, too loud, too sudden.

Good. Let him think I'm slipping again. Let him believe he's winning.

I spin in a slow circle in the living room, then stagger toward the kitchen, knocking an empty wine bottle off the counter. It clatters loudly against the tile, the noise making me flinch for real.

Easy, Ellie. You're doing this for a reason.

I sink down to the floor beside the mess and press my back

against the cabinet. I tilt my head up toward the tiny black pinhole camera tucked into the ceiling molding. Barely visible. Invisible if you didn't know exactly where to look.

I let a tear slip down my cheek, dragging with it the mascara Jack hates when I wear. I murmur something unintelligible and clutch my knees to my chest. I imagine Jack at his office, sitting at his desk, sipping his evening scotch, eyes glued to the live feed of me falling apart. I imagine the satisfied curl of his mouth.

I push myself up after a few minutes and start moving around the apartment again, rearranging small things in chaotic ways: a chair turned sideways, every cabinet door left hanging open, shoes tossed into the bathtub.

I don't touch anything important. Only things I can justify later if I need to.

I leave a few more *mistakes*—a half-eaten sandwich on the sofa, the TV flickering static because I *forgot* to change the input. And then, in the darkened hallway outside the bedroom, I set the real trap.

I check the security camera mounted near the front door. It's still active, still recording to its old backup server Jack never properly shut down. I tested it this morning. It works. It will catch everything.

I walk back into the bedroom, keeping my steps unsteady. I tug the bedsheets half off the mattress, let the comforter puddle onto the floor. I glance at the camera hidden in the smoke detector and murmur under my breath:

"I can't remember. I can't—"

I stop, catching my reflection in the mirror. Hair wild. Robe slipping off one shoulder. Eyes glassy and red. I almost don't recognize myself. Almost. But I recognize the steel underneath. The part of me that won't break. Not this time.

I sit on the edge of the bed, rocking slightly, murmuring

nonsense about my mother, about Jack, about being alone.

I lie back and stare up at the ceiling, breathing shallowly, counting the seconds in my head.

He'll be home soon. Maybe not right away, but soon. He'll come home when he thinks it's safe to finish the job.

I close my eyes for a moment, letting exhaustion pull at me. Not all of it is fake. The fear is real. The anger. But so is the clarity.

I roll over and carefully, quietly, slip my fingers under the mattress where I hid the flash drive just to confirm it's still there. I slid it discreetly under the mattress so Jack wouldn't notice it if he happened to check the security footage.

It already holds copies of everything.

The offshore account files.

The surveillance footage.

The fight with Aubrey.

The fire. The drugs. *The gun.*

All the proof I need.

I smile faintly up at the hidden camera lens. A real smile. One Jack will never see coming.

FORTY-SIX

Ellie

The apartment is chaos. Dishes pulled out of the cupboard, cushions off the sofa, chairs overturned. The hidden camera I've mounted behind the air vent is live, streaming in real time to a private encrypted server I accessed through Jack's own laptop. It's angled to capture the entire living room—the kitchen island where we'll stand, set to capture the raw truth that's about to unfold.

The moment he walks in, I know it's working.

Jack steps through the door. He's dressed in business casual, like he's come straight from work—expensive slacks, button-down, the faintest smirk playing at his lips.

"Ellie," he says gently, like I'm a deer trembling in the woods. "What happened?"

"I'm glad you came," I say, voice steady. "I want to end this."

Jack nods slowly. "Okay . . . I just want you to get the help you need, Ellie. Your dad and I have both been so worried."

I stand across from him, arms loosely folded. Not weak. Not furious. Not scared.

Just ready.

"I know what you think," I begin. "That I'm confused. That I've been sick. That I'm unstable."

Jack opens his mouth, but I hold up a hand. "Don't. Just listen."

His gaze flickers around the room. The nervous twitches in his jaw. Jack's knee bouncing.

"You and my father have spent years controlling the narrative," I say. "You kept secrets. You called it protection. You lied and told me my mother was dead when she wasn't. You discredited her. He watched her rot in that place while he climbed the corporate ladder and smiled for press photos and you helped him cover up everything."

"Ellie, this isn't helping—"

"No," I cut in. "You don't get to talk."

The words crack like thunder in the silence.

Jack frowns. "Ellie, honey—"

"Don't call me that." I take a step forward. "Don't speak to me like I'm fragile. I'm not. Not anymore. I remember."

Jack goes still.

I press on. "I read the things my mother wrote in her journal. I remember the truth."

I reach to the coffee table and grab the leather-bound journal, flipping it open. "I found this hidden under the floorboards at his penthouse—like she was nothing but a mistake to erase." I look at my husband, steady and cold. "I found the surveillance feeds. All of them. You've been watching me for over a year. Listening. Recording. Even the bathroom, you sick bastard."

Jack's face turns to stone. "That's not—"

"Shut up," I snap. "Every conversation. Every vulnerable moment. You used it to make me feel insane. And then you sent me to Dr. Kessler—who just happens to have ties to the men who funded Greystone Psychiatric. Imagine that."

He leans forward, voice tightening. "You need to be careful, Ellie. You're making dangerous accusations."

"Am I?" I raise a brow. "Funny. I thought I was just . . . remembering."

I walk over to the far wall, press a key on the laptop perched on the end table. The screen lights up with a blinking red box: **LIVE STREAMING ACTIVE.**

Jack's face drains of color. "What is that?"

"Everything you just said," I say, "and everything you're about to say . . . is being streamed to a private server. Recorded. Secured. With instructions to go public if I don't check in within the hour."

"You're bluffing."

I smile. "You really think that, after everything you taught me?"

The silence thickens.

Jack stands abruptly. "Ellie, come on. This is paranoid, it's—"

"You tried to have me committed." I throw the words like daggers. "You and him, conspiring over lunch meetings and offshore accounts. You wanted me gone before I could remember too much. Before I found out what my father did to her."

"Your mother was unstable, El."

"No," I whisper. "She was inconvenient."

He doesn't reply. I cross the room, standing over him now.

"You should know," I say softly. "I'm not going away. Not quietly. Not obediently. I've spent my whole life walking the line. But this? This ends now."

Jack tries again, softer this time. "Ellie . . . think about what this could do to your reputation."

I laugh. A dry, humorless thing. "You should worry about your own."

The camera records everything. The silence. The fear.

And for the first time in my life, I'm not the one being watched. I'm the one watching. And Jack's about to burn. He stands in the middle of the living room, sleeves rolled up, veins bulging in his neck, breathing like a cornered animal.

I move to the kitchen island, opening Jack's laptop, then pressing play on the security footage of the night he lit the fire. I've cut it to less than a minute, then set it to loop. To play his crimes over and over. His eyes widen as he registers what he's watching. Him, guiding me to the couch, my stumbling steps, obviously drugged. Then he exits only to return moments later and light the kitchen burner on fire. Flames rise and lick the vent hood. In the video, Jack glances around the room, then leaves before I stumble into the kitchen alarmed by the fire, before he returns and extinguishes it like a hero.

"What the hell did you do?" he hisses in real time.

The air crackles. I should be afraid; I'm not. I'm cold. Controlled. Calculated.

"I sent everything," I say. My voice is calm, detached. Like I'm telling him I left the groceries in the car. "The footage, the fake passport—*Julian*—" I continue, "the burner logs, the files you kept hidden under that false drawer in your office. All of it. To the police. To the feds. To a few journalists who've been just dying for a scandal like this."

Jack stares at me like he doesn't recognize the woman in front of him.

And maybe he doesn't. Good.

"Ellie," he says, voice trembling. "You don't know what you've done."

"Oh, I do." I smile thinly. "I painted them a picture. A chilling portrait, actually—of a husband who drugged his wife with Ambien to make her docile. Who installed surveillance cameras to monitor her every breath. Who manipulated her, isolated her, and made her believe she was dangerous."

"I did it for you," he says, voice rising. "You were too emotional, Ellie. Too soft. You cried when you read about kids dying overseas, for God's sake. You hesitated. You questioned the money, the deals. You were too moral for the business. For *our* business."

"You mean *your* empire of fraud, embezzlement, and bribery?" I ask. "Built on the backs of people who trusted you? People like me you victimized?"

"I had to control you," he says, seething. "You wouldn't listen. You wouldn't play your part. Your goodness was a liability."

He lunges. Before I can blink, he's across the room, yanking open the kitchen drawer. He throws utensils out like a madman until—he finds it.

The gun.

From the sink. From *that* night.

"You thought you were a sleepwalker?" Jack snarls, leveling the weapon at me. "That was me, sweetheart. Every time. I moved things. I smeared blood on the counter and made sure you had bruises you wouldn't remember. You were supposed to fall apart, Ellie. You were supposed to beg me for help."

I don't flinch. I see the madness behind his eyes now. The desperation.

"You didn't need help," he continues, the contempt undisguised. "You needed to be *replaced*." A cold smirk splits his face. "Did you really think what we had was love, Ellie? Do you really think I could love a plain, awkward, simple girl like you?"

I stand stock-still, his words a toxic onslaught that tenses every muscle of my body as I look down the barrel of his gun.

He knows he's hitting his mark, so he continues. "Every

moment was orchestrated. An elaborate plan to keep you controlled, right down to our first meeting. Did you really fall for that fated-lovers bullshit? You're more naïve than I thought. Your father paid me to woo you, keep you controlled, and then I got a bonus when you agreed to marry me."

"Why would he think to do that?"

"To keep you safe. He knew you were like your mother. You were a liability to his business, his money, his reputation. All women are. We had to keep you happy and, most importantly, out of the way so business could continue as usual. Anyway, he couldn't have you marrying just anyone. This family is too powerful, El, too connected. The family secrets are too delicate to just have you running off to marry some loser for love." His laugh is as cold as ice. "Everything was going to be perfect, until now. Until you got that invitation and nearly ruined everything," he rants, waving the gun at me. "You were supposed to sleepwalk yourself into a padded cell—"

He's unraveling. I glance toward the front door. Any second now.

"And then Aubrey and I were supposed to—"

"Aubrey?" I raise an eyebrow. "You think she was on your side?"

Jack freezes.

I step closer. Slowly. Controlled.

"I told you. I sent *everything*. And I made sure not to do it alone."

He lowers the gun a fraction. Confused.

"You think you're the only one who can play people, Jack?" I tilt my head. "You're just a con man who finally got outplayed."

BANG BANG BANG!

The pounding on the door rips through the moment.

"NYPD! Open up!"

Jack's eyes widen. The blood drains from his face. He turns toward the door like a panicked animal looking for a way out.

Too late.

The door bursts open.

Three officers rush in, weapons drawn. Jack drops the gun, too stunned to run.

"Hands on your head! Down on the ground!"

He goes limp. Crumples. Cuffs click around his wrists. The officers haul him up, reading him his rights. He says nothing. His jaw is clenched tight. I stand perfectly still in the center of the room, hair wild, mascara smudged just enough to play the part. The devastated wife. The survivor.

One of the officers gives me a sharp nod of respect. "You're safe now, Mrs. Taylor."

I nod, expression soft. Dazed. But inside, I'm smiling. They find the laptop. The hidden camera hubs. The false passport and financial documents. It's all exactly where I said it would be.

Jack is dragged through the hallway in cuffs, seething. His gaze finds mine, wild with disbelief.

"You—" he chokes. "You did this."

I step toward him slowly, the smile now blooming across my face. "No, Jack. *You* did this. I just showed them the footage."

And then a door opens down the hall.

Aubrey.

She steps out of her apartment in silk pajamas, arms folded across her chest. Calm. Beautiful. Vicious.

She walks over to me without a word, then slips an arm around my waist like we've done this a hundred times.

Jack's face contorts into something primal.

"Aubrey?" he whispers, betrayed.

She gives him a long, pitying look. Then leans her head against mine.

"Vanquishing evil isn't for the faint of heart, Jack," she calls after him. "Sometimes there's collateral damage."

Her smile is razor-sharp. Mine matches.

FORTY-SEVEN

Ellie

ONE MONTH LATER

"Thank you for meeting me for brunch—there's been so much going on for you lately, I figured it was best if we lay low for a while." Aubrey's smile is soft. "And I figured maybe you needed some time to process everything."

I swirl the last of the champagne in my glass as we sit across from each other at La Grande Boucherie in Midtown. "I've been on the phone with detectives almost every day since Jack's arrest," I admit. "It's been a lot."

"I bet. The idea that I ruined our friendship has been eating at me. El, I need you to know: I never actually slept with Jack and I never would have. I just needed you to believe that we might so you could see who he really is and not the person he told you he was." Aubrey's apologetic eyes hang on mine.

I nod. "Thanks for clarifying that. And you didn't ruin anything—you just removed the veil from my eyes."

Aubrey's smile is weak. "I'm not sure if Kat would want me to tell you the details, but I feel like I have to if we have any chance of being close. Jack was one of my targets—just like the professor and the Surgeon General and your father were yours. I'm so sorry things ended up this way, though."

"You don't have to say sorry. I understand why things had to unfold the way they did. Seeing you and Jack together was hard, but I'd rather know what he's capable of than live a lie in my marriage," I reply.

She nods, still apologetic. "Are we okay?"

"We're more than okay." I stand and move around the table to wrap her in a hug. "We're sisters—nothing will ever change that."

"Okay," she says, swiping the emotion from her eyes. "I'm glad you feel that way. I've never had much of a family, but you matter to me, Ellie, more than anyone ever has."

"I feel the same way. Actually—I have an appointment to visit Jack at the correctional facility in an hour; you should come with me and we'll really make him lose his mind."

Aubrey raises an eyebrow. "That sounds like fun, but something tells me it's too soon."

"Probably." I laugh, sitting back down and tearing off a piece of buttery croissant and popping it into my mouth. "I like the idea of shoving the knife a little deeper into his back, though. Does that make me a bad person?"

"Probably." Aubrey chuckles. "But revenge looks good on you."

* * *

Jack doesn't see me.

The glass between us is a mirror on one side—an invisible veil he rants into, blind to my face just behind it. I sip from the Styrofoam coffee cup the nurse handed me when I walked in. The coffee is cold. I don't care. The bitterness grounds me.

Inside the observation room, Jack thrashes against the restraints strapped across his wrists and ankles. His skin is sallow, his hair disheveled. He looks less like the man I married and more like something feral—stripped of his tailored suits and power games. Just a man, cornered and unraveling.

"She's the crazy one!" he roars, spittle flying. "My wife—Ellie—she's the one you should be locking up! You have to believe me!"

His voice cracks on the word *wife*, like it still means something. Like he hasn't spent the last year methodically poisoning my mind and body, pushing me toward the edge just to watch me fall.

"She lied to everyone! She's not innocent—she's a goddamn psychopath! I was trying to protect her, *help* her! You have to listen to me!"

The nurse closest to him steps forward, a pill cup in her gloved hand. Jack jerks his head back like she's trying to smother him with it.

"Get away from me! I'm not sick—*she's* sick!"

He bucks hard, the restraints digging into his flesh. He knocks the cup to the floor with a violent sweep of his shoulder, the pills scattering across the linoleum like spilled teeth.

"Just give him the shot," another nurse mutters.

A third one approaches with the syringe. Jack sees it and screams—a raw, ragged sound, like he's a dog backed into a corner. But the fight drains from him fast. The needle pierces his skin. Within seconds, he's slumping in the chair, his head lolling, his voice falling to a hoarse, delirious whisper.

". . . you don't understand . . . it wasn't supposed to be this way . . ."

I take another slow sip of my coffee.

It was always going to end this way.

Jack was transferred here—to the psychiatric wing of the correctional facility—after his arraignment. The state psychiatrist testified that he was in a state of "acute psychotic decompensation" during the final incident. A fancy way of saying he'd finally snapped. The kitchen fire sealed it. That footage alone was enough to convince the authorities that I was telling the truth.

They know now he set the fire. They know about the drugs—how he crushed them into my tea, into my food, into my bloodstream—until I was sleepwalking through my own life.

They know he installed cameras in every room. That he recorded me showering, sleeping, crying. That he watched my pain like a hobby, as if he were a god.

They know about the gun in the sink.

And they know what it was used for.

The CEO—Colton Raines—was never just a random casualty. The murder had nothing to do with me. Not at first. It was a dirty business deal gone sideways. My father's fingerprints were all over it; Jack just did the cleanup. Paid some strung-out street thug to pull the trigger, then planted the murder weapon in our apartment to frame me in case things went south.

They went south.

The cops traced everything—emails, bank transfers, burner phones. Jack wasn't just sloppy. He was arrogant. He thought he could do anything, take anything, and no one would touch him.

He thought I would stay broken.

That was his first mistake.

I feel no pity watching him now. Not when I remember how he smiled while telling me I was losing my mind. Not when I remember the bruises I woke up with and couldn't explain. Not when I remember how he'd hold me after each breakdown—and whisper how lucky I was to have him.

They tried to take me down.

Jack. My father. They wanted me to disappear. Into pills, into padded rooms, into silence. But I didn't.

Because beneath the confusion, the gaslighting, the drugs, the surveillance . . . I remembered who I was. And I gathered every piece of evidence, like bones, like a trail leading out of the woods. I built my way back with proof.

Jack may have orchestrated the manipulation. But he never thought I'd take notes.

He never thought I'd *fight back*.

The security footage. The financial records. All of it. A fortress of truth.

He didn't know Aubrey was part of it. That she came to me weeks ago, whispering apologies, a plan. He doesn't know she slipped me access to another one of his work phones—the one that held every message between him and my father about the hit on Colton Raines.

Jack whimpers in the chair, sweat slicking his temples, eyes heavy-lidded, pupils swimming. He looks up at the glass. He can't see me, but for one wild second, I imagine he feels me there. He doesn't scream this time. He just stares. And trembles. A nurse walks into the hallway behind me. She offers a polite nod as she passes, unaware of what's ticking behind my eyes.

I take one last sip of coffee, now ice-cold. A smile spreads across my face. Because Jack thought he'd committed me. But in the end, I committed *him*. He's the one behind the two-way mirror now. He's the one whose mind is unspooling.

FORTY-EIGHT

Ellie

The door to my father's study clicks shut behind me like the lid on a coffin.

He's sitting in his usual place—his leather chair, his back straight and fingers curled around a porcelain teacup like nothing in the world has changed. The city sprawls behind him in gleaming glass and steel, but the room feels frozen in time.

"Ellie," he says, looking up with that familiar, polished smile. His voice is honeyed concern, every syllable rehearsed. "What a surprise. What are you doing on this side of town, sweetheart?"

I walk slowly across the room, letting my heels click on the marble like punctuation. I know every inch of this place. The scent of his cologne lingering in the air. The subtle creak in the floorboard by the fireplace. The locked drawer beneath the bookshelf—where he used to hide contracts, pills, people.

"I had a few errands," I say, keeping my tone light. "Thought I'd drop by."

He nods and gestures to the chair across from his desk. "Sit, sit. I've been meaning to call. How are you holding up after everything with Jack?"

I smile, sweet and false. "You haven't heard?"

He lifts a brow. "I've heard rumors around the office. Nonsense, mostly. You know how people talk." He sips from his tea and sets the cup back down beside a jar of honey. The lid is still off.

The same jar I replaced this morning while he was still at work.

He doesn't notice. Of course he doesn't. Why would he question the honey sitting on his desk, the one he's used for decades? It's in the same container, the same label. It even smells the same.

It's just . . . a little different now.

"I visited Jack yesterday," I say, brushing imaginary lint from my sleeve. "He's doing well, all things considered."

My father chuckles, shaking his head. "Poor bastard. I never thought he'd actually turn on you like that. Frame you for that fire, drugging you? It's . . . monstrous. I always liked him."

My smile widens. "Did you?"

He nods slowly. "Of course. He was loyal. Smart. Knew how to stay quiet, which is rare in men his age. I suppose prison will be a test of that."

I tilt my head, watching him over the rim of my eyes. "And the CEO?"

He freezes for the briefest second. It's slight—just a flicker of hesitation in the way he lifts his cup again—but I see it.

"What about him?" he asks.

"The man Jack killed," I say softly. "The man you ordered Jack to deal with when your contract negotiations went south. I don't know how you managed to have it covered up, but I knew you'd find a way. You always find a way to escape the consequences by hiding behind lawyers and your deep pockets and endless connections."

His face doesn't change. That's how I know it's true.

There's no outrage. No confusion. Just . . . silence.

Then, finally, a sigh. He takes another sip of tea.

"Ellie, you've been through a lot. Emotions tend to cloud judgment in times like these."

I laugh. Quiet. Controlled.

"You didn't think this was over, did you?" I ask, letting the sweetness drain from my voice. "You took everything from me. My mother. My childhood. My peace. You put me in Jack's hands like I was a bargaining chip, like I was a gift. You let him break me, and you watched from the sidelines."

His jaw tightens. "Ellie—"

"No," I cut in. "Don't. You don't get to lecture me about loyalty or love or legacy. You never loved me. You loved what I represented. A daughter to parade. A clean name. An innocent face to distract from your rot."

He opens his mouth again but sways slightly, blinking.

I watch his throat move as he swallows the last of the tea.

"Strange," he murmurs, bringing a hand to his chest. "I feel . . . dizzy."

"Hmm." I fold my hands in my lap. "Maybe you should lie down."

He squints at me. "You didn't . . . You wouldn't . . ." He tries to laugh, but it comes out garbled, slurred.

"Are you okay?" I ask, eyes wide with mock concern. "Do you need me to get you something?"

His eyes widen slightly. His hand trembles.

"I think—I think I'm having a heart—"

I leap up, gasping. "Oh my God, Dad! Should I call someone?"

He nods frantically now, sweating, color draining from his face. "Call an ambulance—Ellie—hurry—"

I reach for my phone. I pretend to dial. I even put it to my ear and say a few panicked words to no one.

Then I look at him. And I smile. "Sure thing, Dad."

He reaches toward me, but his hand falls short. He clutches his chest, gasping, his breath coming in short, wet bursts.

"I loved you," he tries to say, but it's too late for lies.

I walk slowly to the door, pause, and glance back. He's slumped in his chair, one hand still twitching, the other gripping the armrest like it's a lifeline.

"I believe you," I whisper.

Then I walk out. And close the door behind me.

I open the burner phone, shooting a quick text message to Kat's anonymous email address.

> It is done.

I smile as I descend in the elevator, slow and luxurious, like the world is finally moving at my speed.

For the first time in my life, I feel free.

Not the kind of freedom they sell you in glossy magazines or spin into overpriced yoga retreats. Not the lie Jack fed me over dinner, or the one my father laced into trust funds and tailored suits. This is the sharp-edged, blood-won kind. The kind you take when you've been denied everything.

The elevator dings. The doors open to the private lobby. The doorman nods at me, unaware that the man upstairs—the one who used to own this building, this block, half the city—won't be answering emails anymore.

I step out into the warm Manhattan night, the air thick with sirens and smog and the faint, electric scent of summer. I toss the burner phone into the nearest trash can.

A sleek black car idles at the curb. The passenger-side window rolls down. Aubrey smiles at me from behind oversize sunglasses. Even in chaos, she looks unbothered.

"Everything go down smooth?" she asks, as I slide into the leather seat.

I click the door shut behind me and exhale slowly, savoring it. "Like honey."

She grins. "Told you it would."

We pull away from the curb. I glance once at the tower disappearing behind us, the glass walls catching the city lights like a dying god gasping for breath. Good riddance.

In my lap sits a slim black folder—my father's final will and testament, the revised version I retrieved from the locked cabinet in his office this morning. Signed. Stamped. Notarized. Names changed. Assets divided. It wasn't hard to get him to update it when I'd been micro-dosing him with tainted milk and honey the last few weeks. With his decision-making skills compromised and his mind more impressionable, I was able to alter the inheritance as I saw fit.

One-third to Kat—my mother, long presumed dead, now very much alive and playing her cards closer than anyone.

One-third to Aubrey, who slid through every door unnoticed until it was too late for anyone to stop her.

And one-third to me. The obedient daughter. The smiling wife. The woman no one ever saw coming.

Inside the folder is also a sleek USB stick, containing the access keys to all of my father's offshore accounts—Cayman, Singapore, Zurich. Accounts worth more than I'd ever imagined.

My inheritance, hard-earned and blood-bought. And then I replaced his honey this morning with a final, lethal dose.

"You know," I say, glancing at Aubrey as she takes a sharp

right toward the bridge, "the way he started sweating? Classic. The honey kicked in so fast I almost felt bad."

"Almost," she says, biting back a laugh. "Nightshade. It's the most discreet weapon in the world. Tasteless. Odorless. Slow-building. By the time the body reacts, it's already too late."

"And no trace," I add. "Unless you know what to look for."

Aubrey drums her fingers on the steering wheel. "You know Kat said she used to keep it in the tea caddy, right? Swapped it into your father's favorite brand herself, back in the day. Just enough to keep him under control."

"She's bolder than we give her credit for."

"She's the one who recruited me," Aubrey says, "into The Society. Told me men like our father don't break—they rot. Quietly. Elegantly. And you don't wait for them to fall. You push."

I lean my head back and smile as the city skyline shrinks in the rearview mirror.

The Society.

A cabal of women—sharp, rich, invisible—who erase the predators the system fails to touch. They don't play by the rules. They rewrite them. Now I'm one of them.

"So what do you think about coffee before we head back to Westchester?" she asks.

"Definitely. I could murder a latte."

She barks a laugh. "We should celebrate. That was our last chess piece in the city. You burned Jack. You buried your father. And Kat?" She grins. "She's already booked us a villa on the Amalfi Coast. Six bedrooms. Infinity pool. All expenses courtesy of Mr. Thomas's 'emergency fund.'"

"Monaco sounds good too," I murmur.

"Hell, let's do both. A few weeks of sun, sea, and zero sociopaths."

I giggle. A real one. It slips out before I can stop it. Then she joins me.

We laugh like schoolgirls—like sinners in church—speeding down the freeway with windows down and the city fading behind us. We're not running. We're *ascending*.

Aubrey throws on music—something poppy, reckless, glittering with sugar and filth. We both start singing along, off-key and loud, with the kind of joy that only comes after you've survived hell and then set it on fire.

I glance at her as she drives, her hair whipping in the wind. "You know what I keep thinking?"

"What?"

"That for all their plans, their networks, their secrets . . ." I trail off.

She raises a brow. "Yeah?"

"They never thought we'd work together."

Aubrey laughs. "They never thought we'd *win*."

I settle back in my seat, watching the stars emerge one by one in the black velvet sky.

And I smile. A real one this time. Because we did more than win. We rewrote the ending. And the city? It's cleaner now. Safer. A little quieter. We left it better than we found it.

And we're not done yet.

Not even close.

ACKNOWLEDGMENTS

I am so grateful for my editor, Andrea Walker, and the rest of the publishing team at Harper Perennial who helped bring this story to life. *Society Women* wouldn't have been possible without their patience, guidance, and support. And to Podium, for believing in the Influencer series and for their dedication to reaching more readers.

Endless gratitude goes to my family for their unwavering support and cheerleading, and to David especially for always believing in me, even when I didn't.

To my author friends: Nelle Lamarr, Andrea Johnston, Robyn Harding, Tarryn Fisher, Christopher Cosmos, Kiersten Modglin, Freida McFadden, Caroline Kepnes, AR Torre, Katie Ashley, Skye Warren, Shanora Williams, Erin A. Craig, Lucinda Berry, Natasha Preston, and countless more. Your support and steady presence has pushed me forward and inspired me in ways I can never thank you enough for. I wouldn't be here without the community you've given me. And a special shout-out goes to a few readers who have been with me from the beginning: Marlene, Donna, and Sally—I don't have enough words to express my gratitude for all you've given me.

To my kids: I'm sorry I wasn't always the mom you wanted, for showing up too many mornings with jet lag after yet another book signing or ordering takeout *again* after playing with the characters in my head all day. You're the greatest gift of my life, and I can only hope my journey inspires you to chase that thing inside of you that you can't see. Fear is the only thing that can stop you from chasing your dreams. Listen to your heart and go in the direction of joy and meaning. Your destiny, just like your light, is so bright.

I also want to thank me for believing in me, for doing all the hard work, for never quitting, for rarely taking days off, for trusting my instincts when so many others didn't, and for having the discipline and determination to alchemize my dreams to reality.

As always, thanks goes to the crew at Aldea Coffee for putting up with me haunting the café every day, asking weird questions, shamelessly eavesdropping, and caffeinating me to within an inch of my life so the words would get written. Your joyous smiles pushed me to show up on the days I'd have rather stayed in bed. You've kept me from becoming a depressed little writing hermit (as is my natural instinct) and added more meaning to my life than words can express. You've reminded me that we find ourselves in solitude as much as in community and what a priceless gift togetherness is. Cheers to the next thirty years of fueling all the words with the best coffee on the planet.

And to every reader who's supported me over the last twelve years reading, sharing, and reviewing my books, and standing in line at book signings and sending emails and messages on social media. You've made my dreams come true, and I wouldn't be who I am without you.

x A

ABOUT THE AUTHOR

Adriane Leigh is a *USA Today* bestselling author of multiple novels and novellas. With appearances in publications such as *Vogue* magazine and *The Montreal Gazette*, the award-winning author, in addition to writing, founded a community of internationally renowned book conventions that draw thousands of readers and #1 bestselling authors to events around the world each year. She hosts the podcast *The Rebel Artist*, and her books have been translated into French, Spanish, Italian, and Portuguese. She lives on Lake Michigan with her family.